BIODEGRADABLE
SOAP

Also by Amy Ephron

∿

COOL SHADES

BRUISED FRUIT

BIODEGRADABLE SOAP

SOAP

AMY EPHRON

Houghton Mifflin Company

BOSTON

1991

Copyright © 1991 by Amy Ephron.

All rights reserved.

For information about permission to reproduce selections from this book,
write to Permissions, Houghton Mifflin Company, 2 Park Street,
Boston, Massachusetts 02108.

Library of Congress Cataloging-in-Publication Data

Ephron, Amy.
Biodegradable soap / Amy Ephron.
p.   cm.
ISBN 0-395-57227-4
I. Title.
PS3555.P47B56   1991
813'.54—dc20   90-22605
CIP

Printed in the United States of America

BP   10 9 8 7 6 5 4 3 2 1

This book is printed on recycled paper.

Calligraphy by Gretchen Overholtzer

"Barefoot Politician Cheeky in Parliament" reprinted by permission
of Reuters.

"Looking for a Home." Photograph by Dennis Capolongo, reprinted by
permission of Black Star.

"Poison in Air, Soil, Food Stirs Anxiety in Oroville" and "Experts Warn of
Lethal Risk Posed by Acid in L.A. Refineries," © Los Angeles Times,
reprinted by permission.

*This book is for Maia,
Anna, & Ethan.*

"If you were to take a series of aerial photographs over the last ten years of the same spot over the ocean, you would discover two things: the color of the ocean is changing and there are fewer clouds."

—an American astronaut speaking
to a group of concerned Hollywood
celebrities, Los Angeles, 1989

BIODEGRADABLE
SOAP

THE WEEK that Claudia became obsessed with waste, nothing unusual happened. She wasn't sure exactly when it happened but, it might have been when she was making the baby's formula and noticed the plastic lid on the can and realized every can of formula she'd used had had a plastic lid — about 362 she figured, if you counted her first baby, too. She wondered why she couldn't have just had one plastic top, saved it, used it on all the cans and saved the world that much plastic. It was the same thing with pill bottles but then she imagined the look on the Iranian pharmacist's face if she were to take her empties in and try to have them refilled, not that she took pills in any quantity anymore, but still, she knew the way they looked at her in the fruit stand. She'd actually tried to explain to the lady in the fruit stand why she insisted they pack her fruits and vegetables in paper bags. "A million years from now when we're all gone, that stuff'll still be here," said Claudia, pointing her finger at the roll of plastic bags that hung neatly over the lettuce. "It doesn't bio-degrade."

"Really?" the lady in the fruit stand said politely. "I didn't know that." She stuffed Claudia's vegetables into the paper bag and handed them to her. "Most people prefer them," she said, "they don't like to cut down trees."

She remembered driving home behind an old Datsun with a particularly nasty exhaust and wondering why there wasn't a law against it, why policemen weren't empowered with the ability to write tickets for lots of money to people who insisted on spewing black smoke into the air, or what was left of the air, in Los Angeles, anyway. It made her angry. When she got home, she threw away the saran wrap but couldn't quite give up the Hefty bags.

"Plastic diapers are the worst," her husband, David, said as he watched her try to wrap up a piece of brie in wax paper. "Francis says in ten years a third of the globe will be filled up with them." Francis was her best friend Lucy's husband, and well-versed in statistics, but Claudia wondered whether that meant a third of the globe if they were stacked in piles or laid out end to end.

"I don't think I could give up plastic diapers," she said as she watched the baby, Rebecca, narrowly miss her 4-year old sister's head with a copy of *Green Eggs and Ham*.

"Rebecca, I hate it when you throw things at me!" shouted Meggie, stamping her foot and throwing her hands out expressively in the air in a perfect imitation of Claudia.

"Please girls," said Claudia, "Daddy and I are trying to have a conversation. I mean, I really feel I have to do my part, David, but there's only so much I can do."

"Oh well, don't worry about it," said David. "I hear they've invented a bacteria that eats plastic."

It seemed like a perfect premise to a horror movie to Claudia: bacteria set loose in a pile of diapers which grows and grows and GROWS. "That's nice, David, but don't you think there could be side effects?"

"Probably," said David. The following Tuesday he left her.

JACQUELINE RICHARDS wasn't surprised that Claudia Weiss's husband had left her. She was just surprised that Billy Thomas had heard about it before she had. But then Billy Thomas had a unique access to their lives.

"She doesn't seem terribly upset about it," said Billy snapping his fingers in time to the music. "Reach, Jacqui, that's right. Higher now. Up. Up. Now forward. Reach. Reach. Now down to the floor."

Billy Thomas was their exercise instructor although he hated to be called that. Private trainer, he called himself, and, as such, he was in their houses twice or three times a week, depending on their pocketbook, with an intimate knowledge of each of his clients' lives.

"Just like that," said Billy snapping his fingers again to emphasize his point. "That's good, Jacqui, bend your knees. He must have someone on the side. All right, Jacqui, on the floor now. Stomach."

"Or else she does," said Jacqui from the floor.

"Do you think so?" said Billy.

Jacqui laughed. "Probably not." She didn't know what she would do if Mark ever left her. She looked at her own flat stomach and the perfect indentation where her leg met her buttocks. But then she was fairly certain Mark would never leave her.

"Elbow to opposite knee," said Billy.

"What about those little girls?" said Jacqui trying to remember when she was supposed to breathe. "Meggie was always too sensitive, anyway. Damn this is hard."

She wondered who would get them on the week-end. Probably David. And Claudia would sit at home alone. That meant she would have to invite one of them. But which one? Preferably the one who didn't have the kids that day. Jacqui thought that children made life complicated which was one of the reasons why, even though Mark had said he wanted them, she never had.

"On your knees now, Jacqui. That's right. Leg straight up. And lift. I want you to feel it burn. Good girl. That's perfect. Up. Up. Up. Up."

Jacqui could feel it burning. It felt great. She looked appreciatively at the indentation just above her thigh. "Poor Claudia," said Jacqui.

"I THINK it looks a little taco bell," said Kevin Baker. "Do you care?" Kevin Baker was the real estate broker and he was referring to the shiny blue tiles on top of the newly stuccoed Spanish-style house.

"I probably shouldn't," said David, "but I do."

"I thought you would," said Kevin Baker. "Should we bother to go in?"

"What the hell," said David, "we're here." And then, after they'd been inside for less than a minute, "Pass. There's something about cottage cheese ceilings," said David, "especially when they sparkle. What's next?"

"How do you feel about rustic?" asked Kevin.

"Rustic's okay, in moderation."

"I mean it's not exactly third world, I wouldn't do that to you," said Kevin.

In fact it was only rustic on the outside, sort of log cabin rustic, on the inside it was absolutely stark and modern. "It's fabulous," David said to Kevin *sotto voce* so that the other broker wouldn't hear.

It had two bedrooms, one for him, one for the girls, central air, a high vaulted ceiling in the living room with a fireplace that worked and hardwood floors that had been bleached. There was a spa in the backyard, not that he cared about that sort of thing.

"It's all heated by solar," said the listing broker breathlessly.

David had noticed the solar panels on the roof when they'd pulled up. Claudia would approve of that.

"The kitchen is completely up-to-date," said the broker, her bracelets jingling as she showed them through the house. They followed her in a cloud of perfume. "Built-in microwave," she said pointing. "And there's a trash compactor over there."

David smiled. Claudia didn't believe in microwaves. She didn't think they nuked the food but she was convinced there would be an announcement someday of the side effects of microwave. He couldn't remember how she felt about trash-mashers, whether they were ecologically correct or incorrect. "I'll take it," he said.

"I'm glad," said the listing broker breathlessly, "I think it suits you."

Kevin piped in, "It doesn't have a lot of closets, David."

"Closets? I don't care about closets. I'll take it, Kevin. Now."

"That's nice," the listing broker said quickly. "You know," she said, her voice just higher than a whisper, "it belongs to Sherry Edwards — she just ran off to Egypt to marry Kenny Bishop, the singer." She giggled. "Do you want to see anything else?" she asked. "The bathroom, one more time?"

"No, it's fine," said David. "Really, fine."

The state-of-the-art alarm blared at them as they tried to leave, "Rear entry ajar!"

He knew what Claudia would say: That's nice, dear, you have an alarm for blind people.

As Kevin raced over to secure the garden door, the listing broker laughed. "I never can figure out these things," she said helplessly, "but you look like you'll have a better time."

"You're sure about it?" said Kevin when they were

safely secured inside Kevin's BMW. "I don't want you to be unhappy."

The listing broker rolled her window down, her bracelets jingled as she waved. "We'll meet you back at the office then," she yelled suddenly referring to herself in the plural.

"Fine," said David. "Absolutely," he said to Kevin, "I think she's right — I think it suits me."

"Well, that was almost easy," said Kevin Baker as he started the car.

David looked back at the rustic exterior of the house he was about to rent. It looked neat, compact, almost sterile, as though there wasn't a way you could collect too much garbage in such a tiny space.

"Easy?" said David. "I guess you could say it was."

"FRANCIS SAYS that one in every three marriages end in divorce," said Lucy.

"It's nice to know that I'm a statistic," said Claudia, taking another sip of the generic scotch that Francis insisted on buying at the Safeway.

"It tastes exactly the same," he'd told Claudia confidentially. "You can't tell it from Chivas — they did a survey."

They watched Francis messing around in the shed out by the pool. "He's turning off the pool heater," said Lucy. "He says we have to economize. Tomorrow morning when I think he's not looking, I'll go out and turn it on again. And by the end of the day, he'll read the pool thermometer and turn it off." Lucy laughed. "It's a ritual," she said.

Claudia thought it was nice that at least Lucy and Francis appreciated each other.

"What can I do?" said Lucy laughing. "He isn't going to change."

They could hear Lucy's 2-year old, Tracy, playing in the house with Meggie and Rebecca while Lourdes, Claudia's housekeeper, and Elsa, Lucy's housekeeper, kept up a steady stream of Spanish in the background.

"Lourdes hasn't left me alone for a minute," said Claudia. "She doesn't think I can handle them by myself. Even when David takes them out, she won't leave me alone."

"Lourdes is great," said Lucy.

"I know," said Claudia. "Don't say, I don't deserve her."

"You don't deserve her," said Lucy. "What *are* you going to do?"

"I don't know," said Claudia. "I hadn't really planned on filing for divorce."

"Really?" said Lucy, with one eyebrow raised. "What had you planned on doing?"

"I knew you were going to ask me that," said Claudia. "I guess I'll learn how to economize."

"You'll never guess who David Weiss is seeing," said Billy Thomas.

Lucy stopped mid sit-up.

"You know the rule, Lucy — we're allowed to talk but you have to keep on moving. Hands under your sacrum. Legs up in the air. Now, right, left. Right, left. Lara Agnelli."

Lucy gasped, "Not really!"

"That's what I thought," said Billy. "I mean what could she see in *him*? Don't say I said that. But she's such a big star and he's just an agent. A good agent but, keep your legs straight. Claudia didn't tell you?"

"I doubt if Claudia knows."

"One, two, three, four. One, two, three, four," said Billy in time to the music.

"I hope somebody tells her," said Lucy, "before it shows up in the papers."

"Keep breathing," said Billy. "That's right. Maybe you should."

"I knew you were going to say that."

"Now, sit up," said Billy. "Legs apart. Now stretch. Over to one side. Well, if you were in her shoes, wouldn't you want her to tell you?"

"I guess," said Lucy. The truth is she couldn't imagine being in Claudia's shoes. She loved Claudia dearly. They'd been best friends since college. But they never had the same responses. Claudia had always been eccentric but lately with this environmental obsession that she had. Francis thought that it was transference — why worry about your own problems when you could worry about everyone else's on a larger scale — but Lucy thought Claudia might be ahead of her time and a truly important independent thinker, not that she would ever tell Francis that she thought that. Poor Claudia.

"Now, the other side," said Billy. "Reach. Reach."

"Do you think it was going on before?" asked Lucy.

"That," said Billy, "*is* the question."

"If you're calling to tell me about Lara Agnelli, Lucy, I already know," said Claudia. "Meggie told me. Meggie says she's very pretty but she talks funny."

"I'm glad you're so level on the subject. Do you think it was going on before?" asked Lucy.

"Does it matter?" said Claudia. "If it was, they were very discreet about it for which I'm grateful."

"And what are you going to do?" asked Lucy.

"Do? The same thing I've been doing. I went to a benefit last night to save the Bay. Did you know that they still dump toxic waste into the Santa Monica Bay?"

"I sort of knew that," said Lucy beginning to think that Francis was right.

"Kenny Bishop played. He wasn't very good. But it might not be safe to eat fish anymore," said Claudia. "That would be annoying. I gave up shellfish years ago but the idea that we have to give up fish now, too."

"You could always eat freshwater fish," said Lucy.

"Of course," said Claudia. "I didn't think of that."

She hung up the phone and it rang again instantly. It was David.

"Hi, Claudia, I just called to see how you are."

"Fine, David. Not the social butterfly that you are, of course, but . . ."

"So you know then."

"Meggie told me."

"I just want you to know," said David. "I met her last week — it wasn't going on before."

"Really?" said Claudia.

"Really. She came in to see me in my office about representation."

"And . . . ?"

"And what, Claudia?"

"Did she find representation?"

"With someone else," said David. "We decided that would just complicate things."

"Oh," said Claudia softly, as though this, more than anything else, pointed out that it was serious.

There was an awkward silence. "How are the girls?" asked David.

"Fine," said Claudia, "although Meggie's teacher stopped me this morning. She said 'Meggie doesn't know what she wants to be when she grows up.'"

"She's only four, Claudia."

"I know, that's what I told the teacher. In fact, Meggie told me last week she didn't know what she wanted to be when she grew up and I told Meggie that was okay, she didn't have to know yet."

"Well, isn't it?"

"Apparently not," said Claudia. "The teacher says they're making a book and one of the questions in the book is, 'What do you want to be when you grow up?' So, I suggested Meggie just write: I don't know yet. But I couldn't help feeling they thought I was giving the wrong answer. You know these Montessori schools, they put a lot of emphasis on motivation."

"Are you sure we should keep her in that school, Claudia?"

"Don't start with me, David, she really likes it there. Why don't *you* find her another school?"

"Don't start, Claudia."

"I wasn't starting, David. I was just trying to have a conversation about Meggie."

"Were you talking about me, Mommy?" Meggie was standing in the doorway.

"Hi, Meggie. I was just telling your father how well you were doing in school. Would you like to talk to him? Here David, Meggie wants to talk to you."

She handed the phone to Meggie and walked over to the window. She could hear Meggie telling David about the swimming lesson that she'd had that day. "I jumped into the water twice, Daddy, and blew bubbles." And then they started to make plans for the week-end. "Ooh, yeah, I want to see *Bambi*. Yeah, Daddy, I love you, too." She watched Meggie hang up the phone. For a moment, she wanted to apologize to Meggie. She took a deep breath. What *was* she going to do?

L OURDES WALKED into the girls' room. Rebecca was trying to take her t-shirt off. Her arms were sticking straight up in the air and her head was stuck somewhere inside. "What are you doing, Rebecca?" asked Lourdes.

"S'hot!" said Rebecca, not quite able to pronounce it yet.

"Mommy says we can't use the air conditioner because it's ruining the odone," said Meggie.

"O-zone," said Claudia, who had walked in as Meggie was explaining. "The fluorocarbons are eating a hole in the ozone."

"That's right," said Meggie putting one hand on her hip the way she'd seen her mother do.

Rebecca stamped her foot. "S'hot!" she said.

"You're right, Rebecca," said Claudia, "it is hot. What if I take you swimming up at Lucy's?"

"I have to admit that Francis is right," said Lucy when they were safely submerged in the shallow end of her pool in close enough proximity to any of the three girls to rescue them at a second's notice. "You don't really need the heat when it's this hot. But I turned it on anyway last night — doesn't it feel great?"

"It really does," said Claudia. "You have no idea how hot it is in the car now that I've given up air conditioning."

"Yes, I do," said Lucy. "Francis doesn't let me use the air conditioning in the car. He says it's too expensive. I tried to explain to him that you don't get a bill at the end of the month when you use the air conditioning in the car but he says it's terrible for mileage."

Claudia started laughing.

"Don't laugh," said Lucy. "It isn't funny. How's David?"

"He's all right, I guess. Don't you see him?"

"Not too much. I can't really take Lara Agnelli. All she ever talks about is herself. She actually referred to herself as a sexual object the other day."

Claudia started laughing again.

"It isn't funny, Claudia."

"Yes, it is," said Claudia. "He thinks that I don't understand but I do. He thinks that I never drive past an apartment with a sign outside that says F O R   R E N T — O N E   B E D R O O M and look at it longingly. But, I do. He thinks I was sort of made for chaos. No one is made for chaos." Claudia looked over at the girls kicking happily away in their swim rings and splashing. "I remember right after I had Meggie," she said, "and David was out at a screening or something. And I was sitting alone with her in the living room, actually, she was lying in her basket. And, I looked over at her and I realized it wasn't a date. She wasn't going to go home in the morning. And I wasn't going to be able to leave even if I wanted to. It was a terrible moment. And David thinks that I don't understand. I understand. I'm not sure I respect it."

"Mommy, train!" screamed Meggie.

"Okay, honey," said Claudia, "let's play train."

Lucy watched as Claudia swam around the pool with Rebecca and Tracy and Meggie hanging on behind her like a train. And then she dived under the water and pretended she was a shark and they were in her way.

It was late at night. Meggie and Rebecca were asleep. The house was quiet. Claudia was surprised that she didn't feel like crying. She was upset about the Chinese screen. It occurred to her she could have asked David for it, and he would have left it, but she didn't think she should try to hold onto him with things. That was what was wrong with the world, anyway, things, and this endless obsession we have to acquire new things. She wasn't going to start. She'd promised that she wasn't going to start, but the house was too quiet and there was a spot over there by the window next to the bedroom sofa where David had removed a standing lamp. She could watch TV but she thought the sound of TV voices would make her edgy.

She wished she hadn't asked him about the anchovies. "What about food?" she said, realizing she sounded like a Jewish mother when she said it. "You know I don't eat anchovies." Her voice sounded shrill. "Why don't I pack the anchovies for you?"

"You know, Claudia, I *can* go to the grocery store."

"I know that, David," she said. "It's just that I don't eat anchovies."

"Maybe you'll develop a taste for them," said David.

"I doubt that, David. Either you like anchovies or you don't. Lourdes," she shouted, "Lourdes, where did you put the extra set of stainless? You do need knives and forks, don't you, David?"

And then Meggie was standing in the doorway. "Hi, Daddy."

"Hi, Pumpkin," David had replied.

Meggie leaned up against the kitchen wall and stared at them.

"Do you want to sit up here on the counter, Meggie," asked Claudia, "and help me pack these things?"

"Uh uh," said Meggie shaking her head.

"I know," said Claudia, trying to sound cheerful, "do you want to go and get a pizza with me when we're done?"

"Uh uh," said Meggie.

"I'm sorry, Meggie," said Claudia. "I'm really sorry." She could feel the tears well up in her eyes.

It really was the worst thing she'd ever done to Meggie — to take her perfect world and divide it in half. She was upset about the Chinese screen.

"Finally, she looks *terrible*!" said Billy Thomas to Jacqueline Richards speaking about Claudia Weiss. "Keep your knee bent. Flex, point, flex, point. It was bound to happen. Keep lifting, Jacqui. Flex, point, flex, point. She has lines in her face she never had before."

Jacqui tried not to shudder. This was one of the things Jacqui had always been frightened of — that she would one day wake up and everything she'd ever done in her life, every drink, every cigarette, would catch up with her and she would have lines, deep lines, in her face that she had never had before. Poor Claudia.

"Finally, he's moved his things out," said Billy, "and the house looks — keep lifting — like half a house, bare spots on the walls, one of the couches is gone." He made a clucking sound with his tongue. "He took that big Chinese screen in the living room. It's sad, really. That's good, Jacqui. Now, other side. Right leg over your left leg, now lift. Lara Agnelli! How would you feel if . . ."

Jacqui gave a small smile. "Mark would never do that to me, Billy."

"I suppose not," said Billy Thomas, giving her an appreciative look. "I like your leotard."

"Thanks," said Jacqui looking at the royal blue leotard which practically shimmered in places where it stretched tightly across her perfect body. "Do you think I need to use an ankle weight?"

"Not unless you want to," said Billy. "Point your toe. Keep your knee bent. Now lift. She's really a wreck," said Billy. "She's canceled class twice in the last two weeks," he said in a voice that indicated that he felt Claudia, of all people, should not be missing class. "Now on your back. Legs up. Hands under your sacrum."

"He's working out four times a week," said Billy. "The one I'd like to get my hands on is Lara Agnelli. Now elbow to opposite knee."

"I suppose I really should call Claudia for lunch," said Jacqui in between sit-ups.

She would take her somewhere nice like the Ivy, comfortable and elegant, divorced people always feel like they're going broke. The one she wanted to get her hands on was Lara Agnelli. That was where the story was. Besides, she liked actresses. She understood them. Jacqui smiled. She and Billy really did think alike.

"Now, lift your legs up slowly," said Billy, snapping his fingers in time to the music. "On the count of four. One two three four. One two three four. That's excellent, Jacqui. Perfect."

DAVID WEISS stood in the doorway to the bedroom of Lara Agnelli's rented condominium and watched her. She was pulling her sweaters out of the drawers and throwing them randomly into an over-large brocade suitcase. "I don't know what they want!" said Lara Agnelli as she started on the dresses in the closet. "I have long dark hair," she said, sounding particularly Italian when she said it. She continued to stuff clothes into her suitcase. "If they wanted a blonde, they should have asked for Christie Brinkley. They do not understand passion," she said. She stood up and started to pace around the room. "They actually said to me, 'Your legs are too long.' I like my legs," said Lara.

David smiled.

"There's something wrong with long legs," she said. "They are not the fashion?" She pulled her skirt up a little bit. "I do not understand this town!" she said. "I don't know why I have to do this. In Italy, I have lots of work. In Italy, they want me." She slammed the suitcase shut and closed it.

"Lara, you can't just leave because some asshole says something you don't like," said David.

"Yes, I can," said Lara.

"And what are you going to do — sit in fuckin' Italy and wonder what went wrong?"

"In Italy, David, I will work." She picked up her suitcase and started to walk toward the door.

"Great!" said David. "Do you want me to drive you to the airport or should I call a car?"

"I thought *you* would be more understanding," she screamed.

"I thought *you* would be more understanding," said David. "What about me?"

Lara threw the suitcase back down on the bed, opened it and started to throw her clothes out on the floor. "Great, I'll stay here. I'll be a — a housemistress! I'll join the PTY."

"PTA," said David. He smiled at her.

She sighed. She took a deep breath. "It's just too hard, David."

"I know, honey." He leaned over and handed her an angora sweater she had thrown on the floor. "It's just too hard until the moment when it isn't. Where do you want to eat?"

"I don't want to eat."

"Come on," said David, "I'll take you out to eat."

"I'm not hungry," said Lara.

"Yes, you are," said David, "you're always hungry."

"I don't want to be hungry anymore, David. Make me a drink."

He smiled at her again. "I'll take you out for a drink. Go on and put on a dress."

She did as she was told. She picked a simple black summer dress cut low in the back. She left her hair loose. She looked at herself in the full-length mirror, her legs, long beneath her skirt, tan, her dark hair wildly framing her face. She'd never wanted to be a blonde. Blondes were boring.

M EGGIE WAS lying on the sofa with her eyes closed. "My head hurts, Mommy."

"Where does it hurt, sweetie?"

"Here," said Meggie pointing to her forehead above her right eye.

Claudia put her hand on Meggie's forehead. "You don't have a temperature," said Claudia. "Were you in the sun a lot today?"

Meggie nodded.

"Maybe you need to wear a hat," said Claudia.

Meggie started crying.

"Have you been crying?" said Claudia. "Crying isn't very good for headaches."

"A little bit," said Meggie in between some tears, "because my head hurts, Mommy."

"Can you try to go to sleep?" said Claudia.

"Uh huh," said Meggie and promptly fell asleep.

Claudia thought about it and realized that Meggie had said the same thing three days running — her head hurt, late each afternoon.

She went in the kitchen and called David. "She says her head hurts, David."

David switched her off the speaker and picked up the phone. "Did you take her to the Doctor?"

"I thought I would tomorrow. Have her eyes checked. Maybe she's having eye strain. Or else, maybe it's a sinus infection. I don't know. She says her head hurts."

David said, "Maybe it's a way of getting atten——"

Claudia stopped him. "It looks real, David," she said. "She just fell asleep with her little hand holding onto her forehead." Claudia swallowed. She could hear David on the other end of the line taking a drag of a cigarette. "I don't know what to do," said Claudia.

"Do you want me to go with you?" asked David.

"Not yet," said Claudia. "I'll call you after we see Walter Whelan tomorrow. Thanks." She got off the phone quickly.

She called Lucy and burst into tears. "I'm trying not to think it's something else," said Claudia, "but if there's something wrong with that tiny little head, I don't know what I'll do. I have to go now and call the Doctor." She hung up the phone, took a deep breath, and gulped back her tears. She picked up the phone again and dialed Walter Whelan's office.

"Marcia, it's Claudia Weiss, is Walter there? Meggie's having headaches."

"Hold on, dear," said Marcia.

Walter came on the line. "It's fairly common to have headaches, Claudia. Does she wake up in the middle of the night crying from them?"

"Not yet," said Claudia, certain that would happen next.

"Then I'm not worried about it too much," said Walter Whelan. "There's been so much smog lately. Let me ask you something else — has anyone else in the house been having headaches and complaining about them?"

"You mean, do I say 'I have a headache' all the time and Meggie picked it up from that? Not really."

"And David?"

"David moved out, Walter."

"Oh," said Walter Whelan, a very expressive "oh." "Maybe it's from that."

"You mean, emotional," said Claudia. "Maybe," said Claudia, with just a bit of an edge, "but I'd like to rule out the physical stuff first. Could we do that? Can you tell me somewhere I could have her eyes checked?"

"I can do that here," said Walter. "Why don't you bring her in tomorrow."

"All right," said Claudia. "Do you think it might be a sinus infection? She's been having swimming lessons."

"Maybe," said Walter Whelan (or Doctor Walter as Meggie called him). "Why don't you let me have a look at her tomorrow and we'll see. Is 4 o'clock okay?"

"Fine," said Claudia. She hung up the phone and felt relieved. Doctor Walter wasn't worried. It was probably stress. That was it. Meggie was under too much emotional stress.

Lucy wanted to know if Claudia was "prepared" for an earthquake.

"I don't really have time to think about it today," said Claudia.

"You should think about it," said Lucy. "Are you prepared?"

"Physically or emotionally?"

"Both, I guess," said Lucy. "Do you have enough water?"

"I probably have three extra bottles outside, but it doesn't matter, the forced granite hillside behind the house will come down and cover them."

"Maybe you should move them."

"Probably I should," said Claudia. She balanced the phone between her ear and her shoulder and lit a cigarette. The terrible part was she'd started smoking again. David had never quite given it up but, after all, he was an agent and on the phone all day . . . Claudia used to smoke one of his cigarettes after supper but, now that he'd left, she'd taken to buying her own.

"Do you have a lot of canned goods in the cabinet?" asked Lucy.

"A few," said Claudia. It didn't seem to matter how much she bought, the shelves were always half-empty, the way Meggie was always outgrowing her shoes. "I guess I should get some more," said Claudia.

"Do you have a first-aid kit?" asked Lucy.

"No," said Claudia, "I don't."

"I'll get you one," said Lucy. "You should have one, anyway."

"What does Francis say the odds are of an earthquake?"

"I didn't ask Francis," said Lucy. "I read it in the paper. They did a study. 60%, better than 60% that we will have a major earthquake in the next ten years."

Francis grabbed the phone from Lucy. "That's not really true, Claudia," said Francis. "There are extenuating factors. If we are fortunate enough to have a lot of little quakes, it could relieve the pressure on the fault lines and then the odds go down. I wish you could come here," said Francis.

"Now?" said Claudia.

"No," said Francis, "not now. If there's an earthquake. I wish you could put the girls in the car and drive here."

"I don't think I could get there," said Claudia. "Won't there be downed power lines?"

"Might be," said Francis, "better not to risk it. Here's Lucy." He handed the phone back to Lucy.

Claudia was touched. She wasn't ever sure he cared.

"I'm sending away for an earthquake kit," said Lucy. "It's only $500. It's got an air mattress and a little cookstove and canned goods and I don't know what else. Do you want one?"

"I can't really spend the money," said Claudia.

"I understand," said Lucy, "but I think you could be a little more prepared."

"I'm not sure you can ever be prepared for an earthquake," said Claudia. "Emotionally, I mean."

"DID YOU see this?" said Billy Thomas, throwing an open copy of *Health Magazine* down on the coffee table. "It says it isn't safe to drink the water."

"I knew that," said Claudia without even glancing at the magazine.

"It says that we should only drink bottled water," he said. "You know it actually links tap water to miscarriages!"

"I read about it," said Claudia. "I don't mean to be rude." She didn't really want to think about that today. "I have a terrible schedule today, Billy." It was 10 in the morning and Lucy had kept her on the phone discussing earthquakes, she had to go to the grocery store, lunch with Jacqui Richards, then Meggie's eye check, and she really should find some time to spend with Rebecca . . .

"No problem," said Billy. "Let's start." He put a tape in the cassette machine he always carried with him and rolled two mats out on the floor. He assumed a standing position with his legs spread slightly apart. "Hands above your head, Claudia. Now reach. Reach. Reach. Reach. Okay, now arms out to the side and circle. That's good. Circle down. And up. Palms flexed. Your heart isn't really in this today, Claudia."

"I know," said Claudia laughing.

"Stand straight. Now flex your palms. One two three four. And other direction. Do you think I should switch to faster music?"

"No, it's okay," said Claudia. "I'll behave."

"You know, they're spraying for medflies again," said Billy. "Right hand on your hip. Now, over to one side. And stretch. They don't even tell us anymore. They do it every summer. Everywhere."

"How do you know?" said Claudia.

"I can smell it," said Billy. "Don't you smell that sickly sweet smell in the air?" he said. "Where are the girls?"

"At the park with Lourdes," said Claudia. Getting doused with insecticide, but she didn't say this out loud. "Billy, will you forgive me," she said. "My heart really isn't in this today. I'm happy to pay you but could we just pick up next time?"

"Are you sure?" said Billy. "Sometimes you feel better if you just work it out."

"I'm sure," said Claudia.

"No problem," said Billy. He rolled his mats up quickly and walked out the door with the cassette still blaring a Michael Jackson song. "I'll see you Thursday then," he shouted. She noticed he'd left the copy of *Health Magazine* on the table for her to read.

She had read yesterday in the L.A. *Times* about a town in Central California where the incidence of cancer was 1 in 4 and there were babies born deformed. Hazardous chemical waste had contaminated the ground water and there was nothing they could do.

Probably there was something "they" could do, "they" being the EPA, if "they" would allot enough funds for clean-up and allow the land time to readjust, but as for the people who lived in the town whose houses were now worthless and whose children were ill and dying, there was nothing they could do except move away, take their losses, and start again. There were hundreds of towns like this across the country and, Claudia suspected, across the globe where hazardous waste, industrial spill-off and, worse, side effects from nuclear proliferation had made these communities dangerous and uninhabitable. She had always found it odd, something beyond a coincidence, that her two girlfriends who were army brats whose families had been stationed on bases in the '60's where there were nuclear tests had both had cancer before they were 20, both survived, but still. She wanted to move somewhere safe, idyllic, where there was fresh grass and water and there were no signs posted on the beach that said:

CAUTION   SWIMMING IN THE WATER MAY BE DANGEROUS TO PREGNANT WOMEN.

But what about to women who weren't pregnant and children? She thought about Meggie and Rebecca and imagined them living someday in a city enclosed by a Buckminster Fuller—like dome where everything was regulated because the temperature outside had gone insane. She wasn't going to start. She'd promised that she wasn't going to start. Except there were so many things that we'd done wrong.

"Do you know what *you* need?!" said Jacqui Richards squinting slightly, the way people who wear contacts always squint and blink their eyes. "Collagen!" said Jacqui. "It would literally change your life!!"

Claudia looked down at the elaborate French china plate with the small mound of chicken salad surrounded by radicchio leaves and tried to suppress a smile.

"I did it," said Jacqui. "Look!" She pointed to the area around her right eye where laugh lines should have been.

Claudia had to admit the skin was remarkably smooth but she had always thought Jacqui achieved that with cucumber slices and European creams, not to mention a near-religious obsession with hats and the fact that she never smiled spontaneously.

"I have this doctor who's a genius!" said Jacqui. "It doesn't hurt much. Okay, that's a lie. It hurts like hell but it's worth it. They inject each line with collagen." Jacqui pantomimed a needle toward her eye.

Claudia winced. It sounded awful.

"It stings terribly, but the results are amazing. It's not like a face-lift. I mean nobody knows that you've done something radical to your face and there isn't the same kind of down-time. Of course it only lasts a year." Jacqui laughed.

"And then what?" asked Claudia with her mouth full of chicken salad.

"Then you do it again," said Jacqui. "You really do have chicken feet around your eyes."

"I do?" said Claudia. She was starting to feel insecure, the way she always felt with Jacqui, as though she were someone's younger sister trapped in a gangly adolescent state.

"So," said Jacqui, "are you dating?"

"No," said Claudia, "it feels too soon."

"I don't know," said Jacqui, "it might just give you a lift."

"I'm still trying to settle the kids down," said Claudia. "It's sort of an adjustment."

"You're still hung up on him, aren't you?" said Jacqui.

"No. I don't know." Claudia laughed nervously.

"But don't you think about having affairs?" said Jacqui. "I do," she confessed. "I think about it all the time." Jacqui ran her finger softly over her lip and shrugged her shoulders making Claudia believe that she did more than think about it. "I can't believe you don't," she said.

"Sure, I think about it," said Claudia. "It just feels too soon." She looked at her watch. "I have to take Meggie to the doctor. Would you mind if we just got a check and skipped coffee?"

"Sure, hon," said Jacqui. "No problem. I'll just sit here and drink coffee by myself. I love the coffee here."

She was stuck. "I couldn't have you do that," said Claudia. "I probably have fifteen minutes. I could use a cup myself."

The waiter brought them coffee in over-sized French china cups. Claudia stirred a teaspoon of sugar in slowly and took a sip. She noticed the man at the table next to them staring appreciatively at Jacqui. She tried to sit up straight but her shoulders stayed rounded, trapped in an adolescent slump.

"Square. Pony. Star."

"That's good, Meggie," said Terry, the nice nurse in Doctor Whelan's office. "Now cover the other eye."

Meggie covered her other eye. "Moon. Star. Circle," said Meggie.

"Try the line way down here, Meggie," said Terry pointing.

"Circle." She hesitated, "X. Moon."

"That's perfect, Meggie. I couldn't do that. There's really nothing wrong with her eyes, Claudia."

Then Walter Whelan walked in the room. "Hi, sweetie pie," he said to Meggie. He put his hand lightly under her chin. "How are you? Does your head hurt?"

"A little bit," said Meggie.

"When I press it here?" he asked pressing her forehead with his finger.

Meggie nodded.

Doctor Walter just looked at her for a moment. "I don't know what to say," he said to Claudia. "It's consistent with a sinus infection but there's no way to really tell if she has a sinus infection without running an x-ray series. I'd rather not do that. Let's put her on a course of antibiotics for ten days and see if it gets better. That seems more conservative to me."

"Conservative," screamed David when she called him on the phone, "to put that little girl on a course of anti-biotics when you don't even know if she has an infection?! All that Doctor ever does is give them antibiotics. Francis says that there was a report in the *New England Journal of Pediatrics* that states categorically that antibiotics on children are grossly over-prescribed, that 1 in 4 instances are unnecessary."

"Why is everything with Francis 1 in 4?"

"What?"

"Nothing," said Claudia quietly. She held the receiver a little away from her face and sighed. "It's just too hard, David. It's hard enough to be worried about Meggie but then to have to deal with you, too. What do you want me to do? Check her in to the hospital and have a sinus series done and then a CAT scan? That hardly seems conservative to me."

"It seems more conservative than giving her medicine which she might not need."

"And what about the trauma of having a series of x-rays done on her head?"

"Everyone's always so goddamn worried about the emotional effect of everything on Meggie—"

"Maybe if you were more worried about the emotional effect of things. . . . Forget it, David. You don't have anything to say about this. She's taking antibiotics." And Claudia hung up the phone.

"Do you think you can manage to give Meggie these?" said Claudia handing David the bottle of antibiotics. "Four times a day? That shouldn't be too hard, David," said Claudia.

"My head hurts," said Meggie.

"You'll be fine," said Claudia. "You probably just need a nap."

"I don't wa-ant to go!" screamed Rebecca.

"It's okay, sweetie, you're just going to spend the weekend with Meggie at your father's."

"I wa-ant my mommy!" she screamed as David carried her down the stairs.

He took the girls out for pizza and then for ice cream and they both, thankfully, fell asleep in the car on the way home. He carried them into the house and put them to bed without brushing their teeth. That was Friday.

On Saturday he took them out for pancakes, then to his partner's house swimming, which was fine, exhausting but fine, until Saturday night when Lara came over and cooked them dinner, pasta with a fresh tomato and basil sauce, and Meggie didn't like it a bit.

"Yucch!" said Meggie making a terrible face as Lara set the plate down in front of her. "I only like plain pasta," she said.

"Just try it, Meggie," said David.

Meggie shook her head.

"It's okay, David, I'll wash it off," said Lara, "and put butter on it. Would you like that, Meggie?"

Meggie shrugged and ran off to get a Barbie.

"I'll do it," said David and went into the kitchen to rinse the pasta.

"That's my chair!" said Meggie when Lara sat down in the chair at the head of the table.

"That's not very nice, Meggie," David shouted from the kitchen. "Lara's our guest."

"That's *my* placemat!" said Meggie enunciating every syllable.

Rebecca watched from her high chair fascinated as Meggie ran over and grabbed the placemat from in front of Lara. "It's mine!" Meggie shouted.

Lara got up and stood there bemused.

"Say you're sorry," said David.

"Not sorry!" said Meggie.

"I think I should go, David," said Lara. "I think they need to be alone with you."

Rebecca, at precisely this moment, stood up in her high chair and attempted a half-gainer off the side. As David raced across the dining room to catch Rebecca before she hit the floor, Lara slung her shoulder bag over her arm and walked out.

As the front door slammed shut, Meggie smiled a kind of Cheshire cat smile from the head of the table. "I'm hungry, Daddy," she said. "Can we eat now?"

Davi d couldn't reach Lara that night, always her machine—I'm not in now, Ciao. When he reached her the next morning, all she would say was, "It's all right, David, a little more than I'd bargained for." She didn't say where she had been the night before.

"I'll see you tonight then," said David.

"Ciao," said Lara.

It rained all morning. The girls stayed on the bed watching cartoons and eating bagels with cream cheese. Then, at 1 o'clock, he asked if they wanted to go home.

"Oh boy!" shouted Meggie jumping up and down on the sofa. "We're going home, Rebecca!"

David tried not to be hurt by this. He packed up their toys and clothes then noticed, as he bundled them out the door, that the living room ceiling was starting to leak. "Look, Daddy!" said Rebecca pointing as huge drops of water splashed on the floor. David ran into the kitchen, grabbed the spaghetti pot and shoved it under the leak.

"Sounds funny!" said Rebecca as the rivulets of water landed with a metallic ping.

"Rebecca stinks," said Meggie.

David changed Rebecca's diaper and by the time he strapped them safely into the back of the Grand Wagoneer, the rain had stopped. He slammed a copy of "Rock Around The Mouse" into the tape deck and drove the half a mile down the canyon to Claudia's.

He made a sharp right turn into the driveway and the car phone rang.

"Your phone's ringing, Daddy," said Meggie.

"No, it's not," said David. "It's got this new trick, every time I make a right turn, it rings once."

Meggie made a funny face. "You really should get that fixed, Daddy," she said.

"I know," said David.

The garage door was open and he could see that the garage was half full with old newspapers, empty aluminum cans and plastic milk bottles. Claudia was inside the garage with her hair pulled back and her jeans rolled up trying to sort out the mess. "I thought it would be a good idea to recycle," she said. "But I never seem to get to the recycling center," she sighed, eyeing the back of his jeep.

"Forget it, Claudia."

"Oh, great!" said Claudia. "I'll do it myself!" She started hauling newspapers out of the garage and David knew he was stuck. A half hour later, the back of the jeep was full, stuffed with old newspapers, empty aluminum cans and plastic milk bottles. He made a sharp right turn into the parking lot of the Alpha Beta and the car phone rang once. He pulled up to the recycling center and a disembodied voice crackled at him over a speaker: The recycling center is closed. Our hours are Tuesday thru Saturday, 11–4. The recycling center is closed. . . .

Great! It was Sunday, by Tuesday he imagined he would have a bug infestation in the rear of the jeep. He pulled into the Safeway, but their recycling center was closed, as well.

"Eet smells funny in here," said Lara when he picked her up to take her to the party.

"I know," said David, "Claudia convinced me to recycle."

"You don't really expect me to ride in that?!"

"Would you rather take your car?" asked David.

"No, it's all right," said Lara climbing into the front seat of the Grand Wagoneer. But he could tell it really wasn't. He made a sharp right turn at her corner and the car phone rang.

"Your phone's ringing," said Lara.

"No," said David, "it's not. It's got this new trick, every time I make a right turn it rings—but no one's there."

"You really should get that fixed," said Lara.

"I'm not sure I should be doing this," said Claudia from the backseat of the car. "The kids just got home from spending the week-end with David . . ."

"It's quarter of 8, Claudia, they'll be asleep in fifteen minutes," said Lucy. "Lourdes is with them. They seemed perfectly happy."

"I'm not sure I'm ready to go to a party!"

"It should be fun," said Francis. "It's at the home of the Swedish consul."

"The food should be good anyway," said Lucy.

"We don't have to stay long if you don't want to," said Francis. "It's for Lasse Holstrom."

"Oh," said Claudia, "I liked his movie."

The house was staid, almost antiseptic, Swedish moderne furniture and immaculate rugs. There were a lot of waiters with silver trays on which were small slivers of salmon on toast with capers, little bitty herrings, and something pink that Claudia thought resembled pickled turnips. The Swedes were tall with perfect posture. She couldn't tell which one was Lasse Holstrom but she thought he was not as tall as the others. She wanted to meet him but she didn't want to approach him as though she were a fan. The guests were a weird combination of Saab dealers and people from the movie business. It did not occur to her to think that David would be there.

She saw him first, from the back. She would recognize

his back anywhere, that, and the fact that he was wearing the same shirt he had on a few hours before when he'd dropped off Meggie and Rebecca. He had his arm around a woman. She knew before she heard her voice that it was Lara Agnelli, practically naked in a sleeveless black dress cut low in back with a slit up the side, and perfect hair that fell sort of wild down her back. And young. That was the part that bothered her, that she was young and very beautiful.

It was bound to happen. Claudia told herself that it was bound to happen eventually that they would run into each other at a party but she found herself wishing terrible things, things she didn't think she had the capacity for, that Lara would be erased from the earth, wither and die after suffering great humiliation, and variations on the same. She wasn't surprised by the intensity of her feeling but by the intensity of her hurt. She felt awkward and out of place. She'd worn the wrong dress. She should have worn the rust colored one cut above the knee. She took a sip of champagne but it tasted metallic, like an old instrument that had been left out in the rain. And then he turned and saw her. She forced herself to smile, a kind of combative smile almost daring him to talk to her. She saw him lean in and whisper something to Lara who turned and looked at her, as well. Claudia gave her a really dirty look and turned away only to confront Jacqui Richards who was swallowing a raw clam.

"Surrendering the field?" said Jacqui.

"You could say that," said Claudia and hurried over to the bar. She lit a cigarette.

"This wasn't my best idea, was it?" said Lucy who rushed up a little out of breath.

"Not your best," said Claudia.

"Do you want to leave?"

"If you and Francis wouldn't mind."

"No," said Lucy, "I'll get him."

She cried in the backseat of their car on the way home.

"WHAT'S WRONG?" said Lucy. "You sound terrible. Is it last night?"

"No. It's everything. I don't know," said Claudia. "The man from the gas company smokes. I was looking out the window this morning and the man from the gas company pulled up and he had a cigarette hanging from his mouth. Doesn't that seem a little dangerous to you, as though it could cause an EXPLOSION? It's probably even dangerous to him, you know, like radon gas. Did you know if you have radon in your house and you smoke, the possibility of cancer increases geometrically."

"Everything increases geometrically, these days," said Lucy. "What else is wrong?"

"I couldn't sleep last night," said Claudia.

"I'm not surprised," said Lucy.

"No," said Claudia, "it wasn't that. The helicopters kept me up."

"Yeah, us, too," said Lucy.

"I watched them out the picture window," said Claudia. "It was eerie—those black helicopters with their flashing green lights, dropping malathion on the city. It was almost as though we were under siege. What does a medfly look like, anyway?" said Claudia. "You know, they actually said on the news, 'Pregnant women should consult their doctors.' And then what? Hold their breath for the next two days? You know, it's not exactly like aspirin where you can refuse to take it."

Lucy laughed.

"I wasn't sure if I should let the girls go out today. I mean, if it ruins the paint on your car . . . ?! David says I'm too upset about this. Why is it I always feel like I'm having a rational response . . . and no one else is?"

DAVID WEISS tried to reach Kevin Baker, the real estate broker, at home but his machine answered. He tried him at the office but they said he was at a showing. He tried him in the car but the line was busy. David Weiss had just had a conversation with his landlord (although the term made her seem too responsible), that went something like this.

"Sherry, I think it's really terrible you're having problems with Kenny . . ."

". . . You can't handle anything at all, I understand that," said David, "but the living room ceiling collapsed and I don't think it's unreasonable of me to expect you to get it fixed . . ."

". . . Yes, I think it's terrible your husband decided to do a concert in South Africa . . ."

". . . Yes, I always thought Kenny had perfectly correct politics, too . . ."

". . . Sherry, could you find a roofer and a plasterer and get them up to the house today because they say it's supposed to rain again tomorrow . . ."

". . . Boycott? What?"

". . . South Africa?"

". . . Yes, I know, Sherry."

He hung up the phone and realized it was hopeless. He didn't understand why it was his curse to be surrounded by women who cared more about causes than anything else. That was what he liked about Lara—she was completely self-obsessed and he didn't think she'd ever had an altruistic thought in her life. He heard the rain start again outside, that metallic ping as it brushed against his hotel window. He tried Kevin Baker's car phone again. Still busy. It was 9:30 in the morning, he was late for work, and, already, he had a headache.

Last night had been terrible. It always upset him to see Claudia. And, then, he thought Lara would have been jubilant after she had driven Claudia away from the party but she wasn't.

"I told you, David, I don't want to be part of this," said Lara.

"Part of what?"

"Part of your divorce. Would you take me home, please."

The stench had practically overwhelmed them as soon as they opened the car door, Claudia's recycling, the sickening smell of old newsprint soaked in sour milk and rotting vegetation.

"Eet really smells terrible in here," said Lara.

"I know," said David, who couldn't help but think that Claudia had done this to him on purpose. It was pouring rain again, so, they couldn't even keep the windows down.

They pulled up in front of her townhouse. "Wait, I have an umbrella," said David. But Lara was already out of the car and halfway up the drive.

He made a sharp right turn at her corner and the car phone rang again once. He answered it but no one was there. He slammed it down again. He thought about leaving it off the hook but imagined a disembodied voice coming over the receiver, "There appears to be a receiver off the hook . . ."

It was raining so hard he could hardly see. There had been a slide at the foot of his driveway and he had to switch to four-wheel drive to get up to the house. He was half-drenched by the time he opened the door, only to find that it wasn't much better inside—right over the place where he'd left the spaghetti pot, the living room ceiling had collapsed and, in a mess of plaster and fallen paint chips, it was raining on the floor, which was when, feeling fairly pathetic, he'd driven to the Chateau Marmont and checked in.

He'd spent a long time standing in the window of his hotel room watching the Marlboro Man towering 30 feet above Sunset as the rain fell. He thought about Claudia's favorite billboard, on Ventura Boulevard, white letters on a blue background, almost as though they were floating in the sky, V I S U A L I Z E W O R L D P E A C E. He finally went to sleep around 4.

There, it was ringing now.

"Kevin, hi, it's David. I'm really sorry to bother you but I came home last night and the roof had fallen in . . ."

". . . The living room ceiling collapsed from the rain, I couldn't even get in the fucking door. I had to check into the Chateau."

". . . I know. I hate the Chateau, too, but they're nice to me. Anyway, I just got off the phone with Sherry Edwards. And she's having problems with Kenny . . ."

". . . Kenny Bishop, her husband. The rock star, you know . . ."

". . . It seems he agreed to do a concert in South Africa. Don't laugh. And it didn't sound to me like she was going to get it together to find a repairman in the next week. Could you? Find a repairman. I'll just bill her for it but I'm sort of out of my element with this and I thought you might know someone."

"No problem, David," said Kevin Baker. "It's handled. I'll get someone up there this afternoon if the rain breaks.

But David, what have you decided to do about the other house?"

"I haven't decided anything about the other house," said David. He sort of thought of the other house as Claudia's.

"It's a very good time to sell," said Kevin. "I don't think the market's going to get much higher."

"You're probably right, Kevin," he said, "but I don't think we want to sell." He hung up the phone and spent a long time looking out the window at the Marlboro Man towering 30 feet above Sunset as the rain fell.

"I HEAR David Weiss is living at the Chateau again," said Jacqui Richards from a prone position with one leg hyper-extended in the air and flexing. There was salsa music playing in the background. "You don't think," she smiled, "he's having problems with Lara Agnelli now, do you?"

"Keep your toe pointed. Straight calf," said Billy Thomas. "They weren't living together. Good girl. Point that toe. His living room ceiling collapsed from the rain."

Jacqui Richards laughed. "That's funny," she said.

"Why?" said Billy Thomas.

"I don't know," said Jacqui. "It just is."

"Other side, Jacqui. And left leg."

He noticed when she turned, the shiny blue spandex of her leotard stretched against her perfect stomach. The sun felt hot on his shoulders. Jacqui had insisted that they work outside. It was one of those rare days in Los Angeles, hot, the air was absolutely clear and the sky, the same color blue as the swimming pool. From the neighbor's yard, the sound of the gardener's lawn mower as it screeched across the lawn and a guttural undercurrent of Spanish.

Billy Thomas turned the salsa up. "Keep your toe

pointed, Jacqui, and higher. Good girl. Now, on your feet. Lean over. Palms on the floor. Knees bent. And into the music. To the count of eight. Right. Two, three," snapping his fingers, "four, five, six, seven, eight. And center. Two, three, four, five, six, seven, eight." The lawn mower next door was replaced by the rhythmic chopping of hedge clippers. She really had a terrific ass.

"And center again. Two, three, four, five, six, seven, eight. And right. Two, three . . ."

He couldn't help it. He walked over behind her and put his arms around her waist, still snapping his fingers, and started to bend his knees into hers.

"And left, two, three, four, five, six, seven, eight. That's good, Jacqui. Perfect," whispered Billy Thomas into her ear.

And then his hand was on her breast. With his other hand, he slid the top of her leotard down lower until she could feel the warmth of the sun on her breasts. He whispered softly into her ear, "Three, four, five, six, seven, eight."

The salsa in the background, maracas and a woman singing about a Brazilian night.

She reached her hand around and he felt her nails digging into his thigh, just below the buttocks, and then moved slowly to the front and stayed there. He felt her pivot slightly.

She stood up, arching her back as she turned to face him, her muscles taut and yielding where she pressed against him. As if in punctuation, the steady chopping of the hedge clippers from the house next door, as the salsa got more insistent in the background.

CLAUDIA WAS TRYING to balance her checkbook when the phone rang again. "Hello. Damn!" She'd lost track of what she'd been subtracting.

"Hi," said Lucy. "Doctor Walter just called me. He says we can't give the girls apples anymore."

"I sort of knew that," said Claudia.

"It's terrible," said Lucy. "How can I explain to Tracy that she can't drink apple juice anymore?"

"She can," said Claudia. "You just have to buy it at the Health Food store and pay a fortune."

"It's grapes and pears, too," said Lucy.

"Yeah," said Claudia, "I knew that. And *Newsweek* says we just lost corn."

"Corn!" shrieked Lucy.

"Not sweet corn. That's still okay," said Claudia, "but corn products. Because of the drought this year the corn crop has been infected with a fungus that causes cancer. We can't buy corn meal anymore or Kix."

"I really like cornbread," said Lucy.

"Yeah," said Claudia, "me, too. But how can you be sure? It's not exactly like wine where they put the corn husks' vintage on the label. They think it could infect the beef, that if they feed the corn crop to the cattle, we could get cancer from the beef."

"Then why don't they take the corn crop off the market?"

"Why are they bailing out the S&Ls? It's all the same—a misguided notion of a stable economy," said Claudia. "I should talk. I can't even balance my checkbook. I made a $1200 error. Or, at least, the bank thinks so."

"Is there anything I can do?" said Lucy.

"Not unless you have an extra 1200 dollars?"

"I do," said Lucy, "if you need it."

"Thanks," said Claudia. "I'll let you know. I thought I'd make a really humiliating phone call to David. I mean, it's not as if I've been buying luxury items."

"Just tell him the price of apple juice went up," said Lucy.

"The thing is," said Claudia, "it did."

SHE MADE A LIST of things you weren't supposed to buy any more.

peanuts (and things made from peanuts)
broccoli
cauliflower (she hated cauliflower, anyway)
apples (and apple juice)
grapes
potatoes
corn (not corn on the cob but corn meal, which she
    guessed extended itself to breakfast cereal)
beef with hormones (how were you to know?)
plastic wrap
disposable diapers
colored toilet paper or toilet paper with any sort of
    design
tuna (because of the mercury and the dolphins)
shellfish
berries (that weren't organically grown)
bananas (bananas were Rebecca's favorite food)

She made a list of things she still bought.

peanut butter
broccoli

apples (but only ones certified grown without alar)
apple juice (how were you to know?)
grapes
potatoes (but she served them without the skin)
corn meal (and sometimes corn flakes for Meggie)
hamburger
disposable diapers
tuna
berries
bananas (bananas were Rebecca's favorite food)

It was too hard. She started using plastic bags again. They had a new system at the Ralph's. They tested the fruit for pesticides and marked it "nutri-clean" but they didn't even stock paper bags in the produce department at Ralph's which meant she would have had to bring her own.

She kept the plastic bags folded neatly in a kitchen drawer and tried to re-use them but Lourdes kept throwing them away. She got careless about recycling in general—separating the newspapers but the plastic, glass, and aluminum were more of a problem—she didn't have a garbage can with four compartments, or was it six that you would need? And, now that she didn't have the jeep . . .

She read in the paper about a woman in Pasadena who had devised an eco-system for her garden. Just an ordinary woman who had a flowerbed of succulents and cactus, drought resistant, ecologically correct, and grew, without insecticide, 70% of her food in a space that shouldn't yield half that. The Japanese had come to study her. It said in the paper that the woman had sold her car two years before and rode around on a three-wheeled bike, her response to the Greenhouse Effect. Claudia knew that she was right but suspected that the woman's children were already grown and there was nowhere that she had to be.

She would have been more than happy to drive an ethanol car, especially if there was a federal tax credit for the conversion, but there wasn't and no one had told her yet where she could buy one. She would have been more than happy to run her air conditioner on something besides freon but, thus far, no one had invented a replacement. She didn't know how to live, the way they did in Marin, with a compost heap outside her window. She was embarrassed to admit this but she didn't know how to make a compost heap or what you were supposed to do with it once it was made.

She began to use the air conditioner again when it was hot and sometimes took the girls out for long drives on Sunday evening.

She went to see a lawyer.

"What do you want?" the lawyer asked.

It was the wrong place to start. "Enough money to support the kids comfortably. David can see them whenever he wants, of course."

"I can probably get you half of his business," the lawyer said.

"No," said Claudia, "I wouldn't want that. I just want a clean divorce."

She heard on the news that night that there were traces of dioxin found in children's urine, traces believed to be left by a bleaching agent used to make milk cartons white. She started buying milk in plastic bottles again.

CLAUDIA DECIDED TO start a scrapbook. She wasn't sure why, except she felt that somebody should keep a record, sort of her version of a time capsule. Besides, it gave her something to do with her favorite clipping —

Barefoot Politician
Cheeky in Parliament

from Reuters

ROME—An Italian politician was ejected from Parliament on Thursday after he took off his shoes and socks and stood in the middle of the chamber in a bowl of polluted sea water.

Witnesses said that Fillipo Berselli, a member of Parliament for the neo-fascist Italian Social Movement, was carried out by stewards after he began to shout allegations of government inaction to clean up the Adriatic Sea.

If she had three things to put in a time capsule, what would they be?

A page from her scrapbook. A picture of Meggie. A picture of Rebecca.

Poison in Air, Soil, Food Stirs Anxiety in Oroville

By MARK A. STEIN, *Times Staff Writer*

OROVILLE, Calif.—Residents realized they were in for trouble when an early morning explosion shook the Koppers Co. wood-treatment plant south of Oroville, pushing up a tower of acrid black smoke that burned their lungs and blistered their skin.

When small but unhealthy traces of the toxic material dioxin turned up a few months later in locally produced eggs, chickens and beef, they realized the problem was not going to go away.

Nothing, however, matched the outcry last week after a 42-year-old woman active in a residents' cleanup campaign collapsed and died unexpectedly at the door of Oroville Hospital's emergency room.

State and county medical officials discount the possibility that Elaine Brooks' death, apparently caused by a blood clot in a lung, is related to the contamination of her family's small ranch south of the city.

Those same doctors, however, know so little about the dioxin contamination of the area—and about the effects of dioxin itself, a toxin found in Agent Orange and blamed by many Vietnam veterans for a variety of disorders, from cancer to birth defects—that the physicians' assurances only fueled the controversy they sought to quell.

Everyone knows there are poisons on the ground in Oroville, and poisons in the air; poisons in the animals and poisons in the produce.

Please see DIOXIN, Page 3

Experts Warn of Lethal Risk Posed by Acid in L.A. Refineries

By JEFFREY L. RABIN,
Times Staff Writer

An environmentalist and a research scientist told a legislative hearing Wednesday that use of acutely toxic hydrofluoric acid at Los Angeles-area oil refineries poses a potentially deadly threat to nearby residents.

"Most of us live in blissful ignorance of the kind of hazards we are exposed to," said Fred Millar of the Environmental Policy Institute, a nonprofit group based in Washington. He warned that accidental release of the acid could cause as great a danger as the gas cloud from a Union Carbide plant that claimed the lives of 2,800 people at Bhopal, India, in December, 1984.

"We haven't had a Bhopal partly because of pure luck in terms of the way the wind was blowing," Millar said, referring to a hydrofluoric acid accident last October in Texas City, Tex.

> ## 'Most of us live in blissful ignorance of the kind of hazards we are exposed to.'
>
> —**Fred Millar,**
> Environmental
> Policy Institute

Ronald R. Koopman, a research scientist for the Lawrence Livermore National Laboratory who has been conducting industry-sponsored tests on the chemical in the Nevada desert, painted a bleak picture of federal response to his 2-year-old research.

meggie

Rebecca

It was 11 o'clock in the morning. Meggie and Rebecca's cereal bowls were still on the table, the remnants of a Barbie-hot-dog-stand, plastic pieces in various states of disarray, were scattered across the living room floor with something that looked like Ken's head (Claudia didn't know why every Ken she'd ever bought had lost its head), there was a fine ash of potato chip crumbs under their drawing table along with pieces of crayons and a wad of hardened play-doh stuck to the floor. Lourdes, Claudia's housekeeper, was a wreck. She was flying to El Salvador in the morning, as she had finally been approved for her green card.

"Are you sure you're going to be okay without me, Mrs. Claudia?" asked Lourdes as she tripped over the castle Meggie had been building for three days and sent the colored blocks sprawling across the living room floor.

As Meggie shrieked, "My castle!" in the background, Claudia said, "I'm sure, I'll be okay." But she wasn't sure Lourdes was going to be okay without her. "I wish I could go with you," said Claudia.

She remembered, three years before, when she had taken Lourdes to the immigration lawyer in Century City for the first time and, as Meggie played with a basket of wind-up toys on the floor, Lourdes told them the story of how she got into the country.

She took a bus. Stuck in Tijuana, she couldn't find a coyote, she took a bus. Of course, she got arrested when she got off the bus. In Arizona. And thrown into an immigration jail. She made a friend in jail whose family posted her bond, got a job, paid her friend's family back, never showed up for her court appearance, and here she was.

Actually, it was a great way to get into the country, according to the immigration lawyer, except the INS had her date of entry. One week after the cut-off date for Amnesty. And it was clear immigration jail hadn't been a great place to be. And Claudia knew what it had been like for Lourdes since, always living with the fear that they would come for her. How she trembled when a stranger showed up at the door and had hidden when an agent from the IRS had shown up to check on a French director who was a client of David's even though she knew the difference between the IRS and the INS.

"I really wish I could go with you," Claudia said again as she leaned over to help Lourdes pick up the colored blocks from the floor.

"No, you don't," said Lourdes. "Someday, I'd like to take you to my country but not now."

"Mommy! Daddy's home!" screamed Meggie, as she ran to the door to let him in.

"Wait for me!" Rebecca wailed behind her.

"I'm waiting!" said Meggie, stamping her foot impatiently.

"Daddy!" they screamed as they opened the door.

"Hi, girls," said David as he picked them both up in his arms, kissed them, and put them down again.

"Hi, Claudia," he said. He looked as though he wanted to make a move to hug her.

"They aren't green, you know," he said to Lourdes.

"Green cards. They're really white." He pulled a small pack of hundreds from his wallet. "I just thought you might need some extra money, Lourdes," he said, "in case you have to bribe someone." He handed the money to Lourdes. He didn't seem to notice that she burst into tears.

WHEN THE EARTHQUAKE HIT, Claudia was asleep. She didn't know if she heard it first or felt it. The armoire by her bed was shaking. She ran into the girls' room.

Rebecca was standing up in her crib and laughing. "Look, Mommy," she said pointing to the stuffed animals as they fell off the shelves.

"Where's Meggie?" said Claudia.

"Down'tairs," said Rebecca.

Claudia scooped Rebecca out of the crib and ran downstairs. The chandelier in the landing was swaying back and forth.

"Meggie! Meggie! Where are you?!"

The house was still swaying back and forth. She couldn't see Meggie.

"Meggie!" She ran, carrying Rebecca. The house stopped shaking. There was a kind of heaviness in the air and everything was still. And then she heard Meggie, crying, under a table in the living room that was covered by a cloth. She'd been playing with a doll. By the time Claudia got to her, she was completely hysterical! "Mommy," she sobbed, "I couldn't find you."

"I know, honey," said Claudia, setting Rebecca down and picking Meggie up in her arms, "I know." And then the house began to shake again.

"I think we better go outside," said Claudia, trying to sound calm.

By the time they got to the doorstep, the aftershock had stopped but there were large stones hurtling down the garden wall. Claudia was scared. She looked at the pine trees and eucalyptus trees that edged the house and power lines that crisscrossed overhead.

They played a game, "Thinking about Animals."

"I'm thinking about an animal that's big and gray and wrinkled . . ." said Meggie.

And you can ride on its back and it will take you away, thought Claudia.

And then they looked down the driveway and there was David pulling in in the jeep. She grabbed Meggie's and Rebecca's hands and the three of them ran to the car.

"Hi, Daddy!" screamed Meggie. "We had an earthquake!"

"I know," said David.

"Mommy couldn't find me," said Meggie.

"My dolls fell down," said Rebecca illustrating it with her left hand.

Claudia put the girls in the backseat in seatbelts and then jumped into the front seat herself. "Where are we going?" said Claudia.

David started the car. "How do you feel about Santa Barbara?" he said. He made a right turn and the car phone rang once.

"You really should get that fixed," said Claudia.

JACQUI LIKED EARTHQUAKES. There was something about them that was sexy. The way the air felt afterwards, charged, and an aftershock could rock the entire house back and forth. God, it was hot and everything was still and waiting. She poured herself a glass of lemonade on ice, added a shot of rum to it, and took a large sip. She had on a sleeveless leotard and nothing else. She couldn't wait until 3 o'clock when Billy Thomas got there.

∧∧∧

MARK RICHARDS FELT UNEASY in his office. There was something about the way Century City felt after an earthquake, as though the buildings had swelled and the next aftershock would blow the windows in. There was a faint hum in the air, as though the power lines were audibly charged and waiting to switch off. The elevators wouldn't work and then what . . . ? What about Jacqui? Mark Richards couldn't remember if he'd put new batteries in the flashlight or if they had any fuel for the butane stove.

Maybe they should leave, drive to the airport, take a plane to Arizona. Arizona was far enough away. Maybe he should let everyone go home and shut the office. The

clients would survive if the office was shut for one afternoon. There was something really creepy about Century
City after an earthquake.

∿

SUDDENLY BILLY THOMAS pulled himself up on his
arms and stopped. "Are you expecting someone?" He
was fairly certain he had heard someone downstairs.
"The housekeeper?"

"No, it's her day off."

And then the bedroom door opened. "Hi, honey . . ."

It was *her* husband who stopped in the doorway for a
minute and then walked over to the bedside table.

It happened really quickly. He opened the drawer of the
bedside table, his side, and Billy Thomas was suddenly
aware that there was a small-caliber handgun pointed at
him. It was terrifying how calm Mark Richards was.

Mark was fast but Billy Thomas was faster and he flew
out of bed and began hopping around the room as Mark
Richards started shooting at him. The bullets ricocheted
off the walls and then one connected with Billy Thomas's
foot. From the sound it made, he was sure the bone had
shattered. Jacqui was screaming. There was blood everywhere. Mark Richards stopped shooting.

"I don't know why I'm surprised," he said, then he
turned and walked out of the room.

MARK WAS GONE. Billy Thomas had fainted. She should call 9-1-1. There was no way she could lift him. There was a huge pool of blood on the carpet underneath his foot. It was clear she was going to have to change the carpets.

She needed Billy Thomas to put his clothes on and tell the same story she did. Ice. She could probably wake him with ice.

When she came back upstairs, he was awake and groaning.

"Is Mark gone?"

Jacqui nodded. "I have to take you to the hospital."

Billy Thomas nodded weakly.

The doorbell rang. Jacqui ran to the window. There was an ambulance outside. It was so like Mark to have called an ambulance for her.

"Here." She threw his gym clothes at him. "Do you think you can put these on?" She had to help him put his clothes on.

"I'm going to answer the door," she said, "so they can help you down the stairs."

She saw the gun on the floor and stopped to pick it up. She wiped it carefully on the edge of the satin comforter and put it back in the bedside drawer.

"I'll just say he shot you by mistake," said Jacqui.

Billy Thomas didn't say anything.

FRANCIS WAS SURPRISED at how relaxed Mark Richards was. As though he'd simply stopped by to pick him up for lunch. He looked very Armani. He always looked Armani. In those terribly expensive suits. No tie.

"I just shot Billy Thomas," he said.

"Did you hurt him?"

"Sounded like it," said Mark Richards. "I didn't stick around to find out. I called an ambulance from the car phone." He started laughing. "I don't know why I think that's funny. Would you think it was strange, Francis, if I told you I was hungry? Do you think I could have a chicken salad sandwich?"

Francis called for one downstairs.

"I found her in bed with Billy Thomas," Mark Richards said and started laughing. "I don't know why I think that's funny. Poor Jacqui," he said and started laughing again. "Did you order that on white bread?"

Francis nodded.

"Chicken salad," said Mark "is one of the few things Jacqui knew how to make."

∧∧∧

THE DESK SERGEANT was bald.

"I need to make a report," said Mark Richards, sounding like a lawyer when he said it. "I—I shot my wife's trainer."

"We heard about that. Mark Richards?" The desk sergeant pointed a finger at him. "Right? Huh huh." He had this funny laugh that sounded like a question. "It could happen to anyone, right? You come home in the afternoon, there's a strange man in your house. You thought he was a prowler, right?"

"No, that's—" Mark stopped when Francis kicked him.

"The problem with guns," the desk sergeant said, "is this." He shook his head. "We already took their statements," he said. "You want to come in here and let me write this up? You want a cup of coffee . . . ? No? I don't blame you. Gives me a stomach ache. It could happen to anyone, right? I gotta say, that guy was pretty good natured about it. Now, what time *was* it?"

"It was 2—it was 2 o'clock," said Mark Richards. "I was a little—edgy because of the earthquake."

"We're all a little edgy. You hear about that woman in Australia who predicted it? I bet her business'll go up! You think the Reagans have *her* number? Huh huh." He looked around him. "We're all a little edgy," he said. "You came in the house?"

"The front door was open," said Mark. "That made me nervous. The alarm was out—because of the earthquake. It was really quiet in the house—"

"You should've heard this town this morning!" said the desk sergeant. "Car alarms. House alarms." He laughed for real.

"The house wasn't usually quiet," said Mark Richards. "There's always some kind of noise. Especially when he's there. They always have that goddamned tape on." He stopped, surprised that he had raised his voice. "I saw his back," he said. "I only saw his back. I didn't think, really. It was instinct. By the time he'd turned around and I saw who it was,"—he threw his hands up—"I'd pulled

the trigger. You should've seen the look on her face."
Mark smiled and Francis wanted to kick him except the
desk sergeant did that laugh again. "Huh huh."

"You're just lucky he's being so nice about it," said the
desk sergeant, "sometimes they swear out complaints."

〰

"WAS THAT PART TRUE?" asked Francis when they
were standing outside the station.

"Which part?"

"The part about the alarm being out?"

"No," said Mark, "I just thought it sounded good. It's
amazing how easy it is," he said, "to take on criminal at-
tributes." And then he laughed, in a weird imitation of the
desk sergeant, "Huh huh."

"FRANCIS THINKS the whole thing's funny," said Lucy.

"Francis doesn't think that anything is funny," said Claudia.

"That's not true," said Lucy. "But he says the weird part is, *Mark Richards* thinks it's funny."

"That's sort of mean, isn't it," said Claudia. "They're laughing at her. Poor Jacqui. I never thought I'd say that."

"I did," said Lucy. She dropped her voice as though someone could overhear them on the phone. "Billy Thomas is still in the hospital, did you know?"

"I didn't," said Claudia. "I haven't been here."

"Where *have* you been? I've been trying to reach you for days."

"I — we — I went with the kids — with David — to Santa Barbara for the week-end. After the earthquake."

"Really?" said Lucy trying not to sound surprised. "How was it?"

"Nice," said Claudia. "It was — nice."

It was the way week-ends like that were supposed to be but never were. Usually they broke down on the freeway and ended up in a hot gas station for hours, Meggie and Rebecca on 7-up-and-cheetos-over-drive while a mechanic with a zen attitude tried to fix the jeep but not this time.

It had been hot in L.A., but 100 miles outside it, the weather was perfect. Meggie and Rebecca sang songs in the backseat of the car. They took a suite that overlooked the ocean. She slept with David. Meggie and Rebecca slept, in the living room, on fold-out couches. After breakfast (which Meggie said were the best pancakes she ever ate) they rented one of those bicycles for four with a green and white striped awning overhead for shade, sort of like a cart, and bicycled around the boardwalk. They found a clown who sold balloons and tied them to the front of the bike. And except that they kept listening for the sound of a big bang down the coast, for 24 hours, Claudia felt like she was in someone else's life. "It was really nice," she said.

"And now what?" said Lucy.

"You always ask me that," said Claudia.

"DID YOU KNOW that in some communities, the Japanese separate their trash into 32 different categories? What I want to know," said Claudia, "is *what* they put 32 different categories of garbage in? Can't you just see it?" she said. "A perfect Japanese kitchen with 32 tiny, they'd have to be tiny, right, trash cans neatly lined up on top of one another?"

David smiled at her.

"Did you know—" she said laughing "—this is amazing! There are two things outside Tokyo called *Dream Islands*? What they really are are landfills with a soccer field, baseball diamonds and a bicycling track built on top of them. There's also a pool and an indoor garden, both heated by the garbage-to-energy plant next door." She stopped for a minute and looked out the window at the trees. "I don't know why that sounds dangerous to me," she said.

"It is dangerous," said David, "until recently there was no regulation in Japan at all. They didn't separate toxic from non-toxic garbage. They don't know what's in the landfills."

She had an image of a perfect Japanese front lawn, lush and verdant, that, for no apparent reason, let off steam.

She looked over at Meggie and Rebecca eating (her concession to frozen food) fishsticks with their fingers in the dining room and imagined them, for a moment, as Japanese until Meggie stuck her fishstick in her juice and said, "Look, Mommy, it's swimming."

"Do you want to help me put them to bed?" she asked David.

"Didn't I tell you?" said David. "I can't stay."

He hadn't told her.

"I have a headache," said Meggie.

"You're probably tired, sweetie. You probably just need to go to bed," said Claudia and tried not to give David a dirty look.

He was there. He wasn't there. He was there. Which was sort of the problem. He was there just enough so that no one else could be there and he wasn't there just enough to convince her he was really somewhere else.

DAVID DIDN'T UNDERSTAND how he was such an organized person and he had such a disorganized life. First there was Claudia and Meggie and Rebecca. Then there was Lara who he thought he should give up but hadn't. Then there was his house which had been supposed to be a pristine corner where nothing happened at all. It was only a leak. You would think the roofer could come, the painter could come, and that would be it but it had been the first rain in a year and a half and it had taken three weeks to get an appointment with a roofer. On the day the roofer finally did show up (his name was Bob) it rained, so Bob couldn't actually do any work. He did, however, discuss the roofing business with David. "There's not really that much work as a roofer in Los Angeles," said Bob. "It never rains. Most years, I just do it on the side. What I really do," he said, "is childrens' parties." And he handed David a card that said "Bobbles the Clown" which just went to prove David's theory that everyone in Los Angeles was really something else. The waiter was really an actor or, in some cases, a producer. He'd actually had the waiter say to him in Chaya Diner the week before, after he'd given his order, "Mr. Weiss, do you think you could give me that script back I gave to you four months ago?" He remembered the guy. He'd come in, dressed in a suit, and said he was a producer. David hadn't believed him, of course, but he wondered who made more money, the waiter or the roofer, the producer or the clown?

Anyway, Bob came back a week later and fixed the leak but an hour after he was done, it rained again and the tar, which hadn't dried yet, ran down the front of the house. So, now the leak still wasn't fixed and the whole front of the house had to be repainted. By now, there had been so much rain in the living room that the hardwood floor had to be sanded and restained.

Bob apologized and said he would come on the weekend except he was booked solid with childrens' parties. He came the following Monday and actually fixed the leak. Then, it took 2 weeks for other workmen (non-English speaking workmen) to plaster and paint the inside and another 5 days to paint the outside. Then another crew of older, slower workmen arrived and sanded and restained the wood floors, after which no one was allowed to walk on them for 72 hours. 63 days later, his house was ready. He loved this house.

"I DIDN'T THINK it was going to be so easy," said Francis after he hung up the phone.

"What?" said Claudia and Lucy almost in unison. It was Friday night and they were on their way to a movie. Meggie and Rebecca and Lucy's 2-year old, Tracy, were happily settled in front of a cartoon video about someone named Jem, under the watchful eye of Lucy's housekeeper, Elsa.

"This thing with Billy Thomas," explained Francis. "He's suing Mark Richards."

"Suing him for what?" said Lucy. "Attempted murder?"

"You can't sue someone for that," said Claudia.

"For six million dollars," said Francis. "For loss of livelihood."

"Has he lost his livelihood?" asked Claudia.

Lucy laughed.

"Don't laugh," said Francis. "It isn't funny."

"Has he been permanently injured?" asked Claudia.

"He says he has," said Francis. "He says the bones in his foot have been shattered. I don't know why I don't believe him. It would be consistent with the shooting and yet I don't believe him."

"What happens now?" asked Lucy.

"You always ask that," said Claudia.

"Either they'll settle or they'll go to court," said Francis.

Claudia thought about it for a moment. "I wouldn't like to be Jacqui," she said. "I think it would be complicated to be Jacqui."

Lucy smiled at her and said, "Are you sure?"

As a result of the new *glasnost* (which is what Claudia called it behind David's back), Meggie and Rebecca didn't go to David's on the week-ends (why should they go to *his* house when he was always at theirs?) except it was Saturday and he wasn't there. He was at the office.

Meggie and Rebecca were upstairs playing in their room, a game they'd made up called Max and Maxie where Rebecca was a little boy named Max and Meggie was a little girl named Maxie who spent most of her time ordering Max/Rebecca around. Lourdes was still in El Salvador and the house was quiet. Claudia was lying on the couch trying to read an Edith Wharton novel but the manners of it were too sedate for her mood and she was sure she was going to be interrupted any minute.

"Can we go outside and play, Mommy?" It was Meggie standing in the living room.

"Do you mean, will I go outside with you while you play?"

Meggie nodded happily.

Claudia smiled. "Okay. What do you want to do outside?"

"Go in the pool." The little wading pool Claudia had set up in the yard.

"Can you find your bathing suit?"

Meggie nodded.

"Can you help Rebecca find hers?"

"Of course," said Meggie, sounding much older than she was.

"'tuck!" said Rebecca coming down the stairs with one arm stuck inside her overalls.

Claudia helped Rebecca into her bathing suit, then let her hold the hose to fill the pool up. The sky looked blue unless you looked out over the city and saw that it was really grayish blue with a murky brown line at the top. It was hot, an August day with just a hint of a breeze. Meggie chased a yellow and black butterfly and Claudia was reminded of when she was little and her vantage point for viewing butterflies was the same height as Meggie's and Rebecca's.

She watched them splash in the wading pool until Meggie got bored and ran off to ride her bike.

"Mommy, watch me!" said Meggie but Claudia was trying to read again and didn't look up from her book.

"Mommy! Watch me!" said Meggie again. Meggie had her head turned to look at her mother and didn't see where she was heading and Claudia looked up just in time to see Meggie on the red tricycle David had given her for her birthday pedaling madly right off the side of the ivy-covered embankment.

"Meggie!" She screamed, "Stop!" but it was too late to scream. She carried Meggie to the car. Her head was bleeding and she was unconscious. When she regained consciousness, she was moaning.

"Mommy, what happened?"

"You'll be okay, sweetie." She laid her down in the backseat and put a seatbelt on her.

"Rebecca, get in the car." Rebecca kept putting sand in

a plastic cup. "Rebecca, get in the car, please." Rebecca started to cry.

"I'm sorry, Rebecca. I didn't mean to talk sharply to you. It's okay. Meggie's going to be okay. Just get in the car and jump in your seat. Please, sweetie." She wished she had a car phone so she could call David.

SHE CALLED his office, the service answered. She called his house but the service answered again, the same service. The same service they'd had for years except Claudia didn't feel that it was hers any longer.

"Hi, Jimmy, it's Claudia, David's wife. Do you know where he is—it's sort of an emergency."

Jimmy hesitated—"I might be able to connect you, Claudia," he said and then he clicked off the line. He came back a moment later. "I can put you through now," he said.

"Claudia, what is it?" asked David.

"Did you pick that up, David?" A woman's voice on the extension with a slight accent, the sort of accent a young Italian actress would have.

"It's Meggie, David," said Claudia sounding as cold as she could except she was too upset about Meggie to sound cold. "She had an accident. I'm at Cedars."

"Is she all right?"

"I don't know yet," said Claudia, not wanting to give him any information. Wanting it to sound worse than it was. Wanting him to feel worse about Meggie than she did about Lara Agnelli. "She hit her head."

"I—I'll be right there," said David.

Claudia slammed down the phone. At this point, Rebecca, who was still in her wet bathing suit, was shivering. Claudia asked one of the nurses if she could borrow a hospital gown and she slipped Rebecca's wet bathing suit off onto the examining room floor and tied the blue hospital gown around her. It was sort of big and Rebecca looked like a mouse in it. "I have an idea," said Claudia, "let's play Doctor. You'll be the patient and Meggie will be the Doctor."

Meggie, who was lying very still on her back on an examining table, managed a smile.

"What have we here?" said the real Doctor when he finally came into the room.

Child abuse, thought Claudia, *he's going to think that it was child abuse. They always think that now.* She saw the Doctor carefully sizing her up. *Child neglect, more like it.*

"There's always a lot of blood from a head wound," he said to Claudia smiling. "Sometimes they seem scarier than they are. Did she black out?"

Claudia nodded. "For a minute."

"You're going to have quite a bump on that head, young lady," he said, and pointed a small flashlight into her eyes, "and a headache. I think she's going to be okay," he said to Claudia, "but I want you to wake her up every two hours tonight, just to be sure." Claudia remembered Doctor Walter explaining, "The danger being that they go to sleep and don't wake up," when Meggie fell backwards off her rocking horse when she was ten months old. That time she and David had gone together, every two hours, routing themselves from sleep, nervously tiptoeing together into her room. "It doesn't make any sense that we're whispering," Claudia had said, finally, "we're just going in to wake her up." David had laughed at that. She would be waking Meggie alone tonight.

"It's not as if we're together, Claudia," said David when he saw her at the hospital.

"What are we, David? Don't answer that. I don't really want to talk about it. Will you just help me carry Meggie to the car."

"I'd feel better if I took her home," said David.

"Okay," said Claudia, "but then you have to leave."

As they were walking out through the lobby, Jacqui Richards walked in on her way to see Billy Thomas. She looked terrible. She had a scarf tied around her hair, dark glasses and no make-up. Her face looked tight and drawn. She had on stretch pants, the old fashioned kind that look like capris, and sandals with heels. She looked cheap.

"Is that Meggie?" she said at the bundle in David's arms. "And you must be Abigail," she said to Rebecca.

"Rebecca," said David.

"Oh right. Of course," said Jacqui Richards. She looked at David and at Claudia. "It's so nice to see you both together," she said, and then she added wistfully, "I think divorce is one of the worst things one's friends can do."

"My head hurts, Daddy," said Meggie.

"I don't see why you have to sue," said Jacqui.

"You wouldn't see," said Billy Thomas and he gave her a look that was so awful she felt she was going to have to do something to make up for it.

She sighed. She was sitting in an uncomfortable orange vinyl chair in his hospital room. She still had her hair tied back in a scarf and dark glasses on. There were stress lines across her forehead. She knew she didn't look . . . she wanted to say "good" but "rich" was really what it was. In two short weeks, she'd lost that thing that separated the appearance of someone with money from someone without. She'd thought, that morning as she looked at herself in the vanity in her bedroom, that she was starting to look desperate.

She hadn't spoken to Mark. She'd called him but he hadn't returned her call. He'd done this really Hollywood thing and had his lawyer return the call, a lawyer at a Century City law firm who *only* handled divorces, the same lawyer Claudia Weiss was using (or maybe not using by the look of it). Slick. His tone was like butter that wouldn't melt. "You understand, dear," he said, "if he doesn't want to speak to you right now. He asked *me* to call to make sure you were comfortable."

In the end, it was all about comfort, wasn't it?

"Mark just wanted to make sure you don't *need* anything," said the lawyer.

Jacqui assured him she didn't *need* anything.

"You'll call if you do," said Mark's lawyer, and gave her his number.

It was strange to think she didn't know where Mark lived. They'd been married for 13 years and now she didn't know where he lived.

Billy Thomas made another terrible face as he tried to adjust himself in the bed. He looked miserable. He had his foot up in traction, so the bone could set, suspended by wires and pulleys at a 30-degree angle in the air. The doctors said he would be in traction for another month, already his left leg looked smaller than the other. He winced as he settled down on the bed.

She really was going to have to do something to make it better. Jacqui walked over and shut the hospital room door. She sat down on his bed. She leaned her head down and gently opened his bathrobe.

She hesitated for a moment. "But it's just going to be so uncomfortable, Billy, if you sue," she said, whining a little when she said it.

"Good," said Billy Thomas, "I'd like that."

> *This has all the rhythms of an ecological joke (pretend you sound like someone in the Catskills):*
>
> a bird swoops down into a landfill to try to find a crumb, grabs a crumb, manages to hook his neck in one of those plastic rings that holds a six pack in, strangles himself, and dies.

CLAUDIA WENT to a seminar. She learned that the rain forest was disappearing at the rate of 50 acres a minute; that you still weren't supposed to eat tuna fish; that you are supposed to cut the plastic rings that hold a six pack before discarding it because they're finding that it strangles birds; that the Greenhouse Effect is real; that it isn't safe to swim in the ocean after it rains; that there is no such thing as safe nuclear power; that the depletion of the ozone is worse than previously thought; that there is hope: that we have fifteen years and, if we radically change the way we do things in the next fifteen years, we may be able to stop this mess.

At the seminar, she met someone. She now got to add to the list of things she was guilty about, the time that she spent with Alex.

Maybe it was the way his house was situated on the hill so it seemed as though the wind were hitting it from all sides. He couldn't remember what Claudia had told him—something about the Greenhouse Effect and the wind, global warming having an effect on the wind, and by the year 2000, winds at a speed of _____ (that was the part he couldn't remember) would be common. He wondered how fast the wind *was* blowing. 30 miles an hour? 40 miles an hour? He didn't know how much more wind his house could take. The windows were rattling in their frames and there was a kind of whistling sound in the trees. He shivered under the down comforter with the blue striped flannel duvet cover Lara Agnelli had given him and tried for the ninth time that night to go to sleep. He couldn't sleep. He turned on the Travel Channel, this weird channel Claudia had discovered when she was nursing Meggie and they used to get up in the middle of the night and watch TV, it ran travelogues from 2 a.m. till noon, but this night they were exploring Las Vegas. He turned the TV off and closed his eyes. He tried to practice a yoga relaxation exercise and then, he heard this terrible noise as though something had fallen on the roof and then, whatever it was slid off with a terrible scraping noise and then, there was a terrible crash and the car alarm and the house alarm went off simultaneously.

He shouldn't be the nervous kind of fellow who wouldn't go outside but he thought it would be better if he just waited inside until the guard from Bel-Air Patrol arrived. It was hard to say what had landed.

Solar panels, thanks to Bob, the roofer, who it seemed had forgotten to reconnect them when he put them back up on the roof and they had, prompted by the wind, slid right off the roof of the house and through the roof of the Grand Wagoneer, setting off the car alarm and the house alarm simultaneously and leaving, he would discover later, a 4-inch tear in the leather upholstery in the backseat of the car. David wasn't sure how he felt about the house now.

Claudia found an old can of snail poison in the garage. She thought about throwing it away and then stopped herself. She didn't know where to throw it away. She'd read too much about toxic landfills and acid rain. She kept it in the garage on a high shelf so Meggie and Rebecca couldn't reach it.

She had spent the night at Alex's the night before, not the whole night but enough of the night so she'd actually slept a bit. She'd come home at 4. She didn't want Meggie and Rebecca to wonder where she was in the morning. She hadn't introduced them yet to Alex. It had been strange, driving home at 4 on deserted streets, as though she were sneaking through the canyon.

"You look a little tired, Mrs. Claudia," said Lourdes as she handed her a strong cup of coffee. Lourdes had returned from El Salvador with her green card in a slightly better mood but Claudia wasn't sure what Lourdes really thought of her behavior. She knew Lourdes thought most men were useless—she'd given them up years ago, after her first husband (Claudia never could get it straight whether they were actually married or not) ran off with someone else leaving Lourdes with two infant children, but Claudia wasn't ready to give up men although lately she felt they had taken on teenage proportions, arguing with David, concealing Alex. "Thank you, Lourdes," she said. "I am a little tired."

She had to see David in his office at 3. There were some things they had to go over, where they should apply to school for Meggie, as though it were really their choice, Meggie would go wherever she got in. There was a place on the applications, under PARENTS, and a choice, MARRIED, DIVORCED, OTHER. Claudia wrote, "Separated," and wondered whether that were in Meggie's favor. CHILD LIVES WITH WHICH PARENT? Claudia wrote, "Mother." Under MOTHER'S OC-CUPATION, she wrote, "Futurist."

H E THOUGHT it was sort of incredible that Sherry Edwards had asked him to leave! After all the trouble he'd had! After the months he'd spent at the Chateau! After this recent episode with the solar panels and the jeep! He'd only just gotten the jeep back!

"We're getting divorced," said Sherry. "I don't know, it just didn't work out. Two careers, two temperaments," she said, as though he really wanted to hear the intimate details of their breakup. "I'm feeling a little off-center," she said. "You know, like my head's askew," she said. "It would really mean a lot to me, I think it would really balance me, if I could have my house back."

He wasn't going to give it to her.

"I just want to burrow in," she said, "somewhere that's familiar to me. It's all been sort of awful," she said.

David knew that. He'd read about it. How Kenny Bishop had run off with that model Tammy what's-her-name and Tammy what's-her-name was pregnant. But he still didn't see why *he* should move. What about *his* sense of balance? What about *his* divorce? What about *his* children?

"MEGGIE AND REBECCA are down the street, David," said Claudia, "playing with a friend. Do you want me to go and get them?"

"I wanted to talk to you," he said.

Claudia just stood in the doorway.

"Can I come in?"

Claudia shook her head, "I think we should sit outside," she said. She walked up the steps to the little grass patio and sat at the table. David followed her. There was a little toy train tricycle of Rebecca's lying sideways on the grass. David leaned down and picked it up. She watched him.

"Did something else happen to your house, David?" asked Claudia. "You always come here when something happens to your house."

"The solar panels fell off," said David. He smiled. "But that was days ago." He sat down at the table opposite her.

Claudia stood up. "Is Lara out of town?"

"No, she's back."

Claudia sat down again. "What is it, David?"

He looked away from her. "I just thought—" He stopped. "You might—" He stopped again. "I wanted to see you."

Claudia looked at him.

"Do you want to have dinner?"

"No," said Claudia. "Do you want me to run up the street and get the kids?"

"No," said David, "that's okay. I'll stop by tomorrow to see them, if that's all right with you?"

"Fine," said Claudia. She stood up. She walked past him into the house and shut the door behind her. Her heart was beating, but he didn't know that, so fast she could hear it when she walked. She took a deep breath and listened for the sound of his car door slamming and the engine starting. She walked over to the window and stood, just on the side of it where he couldn't see her, and watched him drive away.

THE GIRL in Billy Thomas's hospital room was wearing shorts. She was young. Jacqui could only guess how young. And there was something about the casual way she stood at the foot of his bed as though she belonged there. In the moment before he realized Jacqui Richards had come into the room, she saw the way Billy Thomas looked at her. Her name was Karen. And, Jacqui would discover later, she was the daughter of another of his clients. She was laughing at the moment Jacqui Richards walked into the room. She had her head thrown back and she was laughing and Billy Thomas was smiling at her as she laughed until he noticed Jacqui and a look crossed his face like a deer that was trapped in someone's headlights and then it changed to a more defiant hostile look as if he meant to say, "You know, now. So what?"

What? thought Jacqui as in, now what?

"I'm sorry," said Jacqui, mustering some "older woman with manners and a slight sense of grace" in her tone, if such a thing were possible under the circumstances because they were really tawdry circumstances, "I didn't mean to interrupt."

"You're not interrupting," said Billy Thomas with that small mean smile again.

"I think I'll just come back later," said Jacqui and she closed the door behind her.

"Claudia . . ." It was Jacqui Richards on the phone. "Do you know where he is?"

She sounded terrible. "Mark?"

"It's really embarrassing," said Jacqui. "I don't know where he lives . . ."

"I TOLD HER," said Claudia. "Can you imagine? I don't know what happened then but I told her where he lived."

"I don't know if I would have," said Lucy.

"What would you have done?"

"Lied," said Lucy, "and told her that I didn't know."

"And if she asked you for the phone number?"

"I'd pretend I always call him at his office," said Lucy.

"I'm not as quick as you are," said Claudia. "The weird thing is, she didn't ask me for the phone number."

"I guess she drove right over," said Lucy.

"I bet we'll find out," said Claudia.

"What are you two gossiping about?" said Francis.

"Nothing," said Lucy as Claudia said, "Jacqui."

"I see," said Francis, waiting for one of them to say something more but neither of them did.

"Have you ever noticed," said Lucy to Claudia after Francis went back upstairs, "how men like to gossip just as much as women do, they just don't like to admit it? I swear Francis talks on the phone more than I do."

"I know David talks on the phone more than I do."

"How is David?"

Claudia smiled. "I knew you were going to ask me that. He was over yesterday."

"To see the kids?"

"No, to see me. He wanted to go out to dinner."

"And?"

"I told him no." She stopped because Francis walked back into the room.

"Did you know," she said to Francis, "that the hole in the ozone over the Antarctic is the size of the continental United States?"

"In the spring," said Francis.

"In the antarctic spring," said Claudia.

The hole in the ozone over the Antarctic in the middle of the spring is as large as the continental United States and as tall as Mount Everest but by late spring ozone levels return to normal. Claudia wanted to know, if, when they reported that there was a 3% loss in the ozone, the loss were temporary (sort of like a temporary memory loss but she imagined a temporary memory loss could be serious to someone who was experiencing it) or permanent. She didn't mean to belittle the hole in the ozone. In fact, she was really frightened of the hole in the ozone. She just didn't think she understood it. A couple of weeks a year, there's a hole and then it disappears. But does the ozone loss just spread itself across the globe or do the ozone levels really return to normal? It was sort of like a catch phrase—the ozone levels return to normal.

"WE HAVE TO TALK," said David.

"About what?" said Claudia.

"About Alex."

She wondered how he knew about Alex. "I don't think we have anything to talk about," she said.

"Yes, we do," said David. "Is it serious?"

"I don't know if it's any of your business, David. Forgive me, but I didn't think those were the rules. Do you want me to tell Meggie and Rebecca you're here?"

"Yes, please," said David.

"Meggie," said David, the moment Meggie appeared on the stairs. "Guess what?! I have tickets to the Moscow Circus."

"Rebecca," screamed Meggie, "we're going to the circus."

David looked at Claudia. He hesitated, "I have an extra one," he said.

She wanted to say, "Why don't you call Lara Agnelli, then," but she stopped herself because Meggie was in the room. "I have things to do, David," she said. "Thanks. What time will you be home?" Meaning, what time will you have the kids home?

"Before dinner," he said, "if it's okay." Rebecca ran into David's arms. "Unless, you want me to take them for dinner," he said.

"No, it's okay," said Claudia, "I wasn't doing anything tonight, anyway."

"That's good," said David.

She wished he'd stop.

"Are you sure you don't want to come to the circus, Mommy?" said Meggie.

"I can't, sweetie," said Claudia, and she gave Meggie a kiss goodbye. And then she leaned over and gave Rebecca a kiss goodbye even though Rebecca was still in David's arms. "Have a good time," she said, "eat some popcorn for me, and don't step on any elephants," which even Meggie didn't think was a very good joke.

After they left, she called Alex. "I'm sort of free," she said.

"What does that mean?" said Alex.

"It means the girls went to the circus. Do you want to—I don't know—go to a museum?"

They went to the LA County Museum to see the Georgia O'Keeffe exhibit and the whole time Claudia thought about Meggie and Rebecca. Lucy had a theory that if you were going to go out on the week-end without your kids you should go somewhere where no one else had taken theirs. Lucy was right. She wished she were at the circus. She decided Georgia O'Keeffe's watercolors reminded her of sorbet. She didn't tell Alex. What she really wanted to do was go home and wait for Meggie and Rebecca. Make them a cake. She was sort of a disaster as a mother lately. She couldn't remember the last time she'd made them a cake.

"I CAN'T BELIEVE Billy Thomas is taking you to court," said Lucy.

"I tried to settle," said Mark. "I offered him a hundred thousand dollars. He wouldn't take it. He won't settle," said Mark. He took a bite of a shrimp toast and handed it to Jacqui. "I think he *wants* to go to court."

"I think he *wants* the publicity," said Claudia.

"I'm sure of that," said Lucy.

"I'm sure *we* don't," said Mark speaking for himself and Jacqui. There was something strange about the way Jacqui sat at Mark's side, with no expression on her face chewing the remains of his shrimp toast. Claudia had a vision of how she would appear in court like Maureen Dean, dressed perfectly in blacks and whites, her hair pulled back à la Chanel, sitting in the stands for her husband.

Claudia was glad Mark Richards and Jacqui Richards had gotten back together partly because she couldn't figure out what would have happened to Jacqui if they hadn't, yet, it was strange to be the odd man out. She guessed she could have brought Alex to dinner but Alex was a mistake and she didn't need him to be a bigger mistake than he was. She wondered if she'd always be alone.

"Can I have another one of those shrimp toasts?" said Jacqui. It was irritating the way Jacqui could eat anything she wanted.

"What happens when you finally go to court?" asked Lucy.

"I'll probably lose," said Mark, "unless we decide to tell the truth. You see, he still says, I thought he was a prowler."

Jacqui got a little pale.

"You may lose, anyway," said Francis, "this isn't Texas."

"I'll probably lose," said Mark, "especially if it's a jury trial, rich lawyer, poor working class stiff."

"And the second you pay him off," said Claudia, "he'll make a trainer comeback."

"Is that legal?" asked Lucy. "I mean, can a person claim loss of livelihood, *win*, and then go back to work?"

"Probably," said Francis.

"Not technically," said Mark, "but the D.A. would have to prosecute him for perjury and that's not likely to happen. I'd rather prove he's lying now. I had an interesting conversation with your ex," said Mark to Claudia. "He had a plan."

"He usually does," said Claudia.

"I'm a little desperate," said Mark, "I'll try anything. Short of force," he added, as though someone had instructed him to add that. "I'd rather not have to tell the truth," he said.

"Thanks, dear," said Jacqui. "I'd rather not be in the tabloids. Does anybody want some spicy eggplant?" she said holding up the carton. Everybody looked at her. "I'm not looking forward to going to court," she said.

"I'M NOT SURPRISED they got back together," said Claudia to Lucy the next morning when Lucy called her to discuss the party. "You know, I went shopping with her the other day."

"You went shopping with Jacqui Richards?" said Lucy.

"You know, I can go into a clothes store," said Claudia.

"I know," said Lucy, "it just isn't like you."

"That's not the point," said Claudia. "We were driving down the street and we passed this woman, this old woman who I think lives on the corner of Melrose and Spaulding with her shopping cart. She reminds me of the bird woman in *Mary Poppins*. You know, the one who sang, 'Feed the birds, tuppence a bag,' except she doesn't have any bread crumbs and this isn't London. Anyway, Jacqui said to me that she can't stand to drive past them, which I thought was a little elitist already, *them*, as though she could lump the homeless into one sub-division, but that wasn't really what she meant. She meant homeless women.

"'I always used to make Mark stop,' she said, 'and give them money.'"

"As though she couldn't do it herself," said Lucy.

"She couldn't," said Claudia. "That's the point."

Billy Thomas leaned over on his crutches and closed the door to his apartment with his elbow—he never was going to get used to the damned things. The light on his answering machine was blinking steadily. The air in the room had a layer of dust. It had been two months since he'd been in his apartment. After three weeks in the hospital, he had developed an infection in his leg from a bullet fragment that had lodged just above the ankle. It had taken two surgeries to remove it, after which he'd been forced to keep the leg raised, up in the air with wires and a pulley so that it wouldn't swell, all of which had put him in a terrible mood and the only thing that had helped was holding on to the thought that he would be rich soon.

There was a stack of unopened mail on his desk. Bills. He was sure they were all bills. There were streaks of light coming in through the levolor blinds, flat light, which made a bright white pattern on the floor. He threw his crutches down, hopped over to the desk chair, and sat down. He looked around as though he expected someone to be watching him. He tried to hold on to the thought that he would be rich soon.

KAREN ESTRITCH looked at her mother angrily. Her parents didn't understand that she was in love. "He's not just doing it for the money, Mom!" She didn't want to have this conversation. They'd never approved of *any* of her boyfriends. But it was her mom who'd brought Billy Thomas into the house to begin with. It was her mom who said he walked on water. It was her mom who'd thought he was a yoga genius. "You'll never understand, Mom. He feels it was a violation to be shot."

"It's not me, Karen. You know how your father feels . . ."

"Basically? That I should stay in the closet for the next six years until I get a Master's. What did he want me to get a Master's in, Mom?"

"That's not fair. Really, Karen. Daddy and I just wish you'd take it slower."

"Tell me the part now about how hard Daddy worked for me. He did it all for me. So that I would have every opportunity. And you just don't want me to throw it away."

"Something like that," said Nancy Estritch. She'd lost her, for the time being, anyway. She could see that. She just wished she hadn't lost her to that New Age scum.

"You always raised me to believe I should make my own choices, Mom."

"That's true. I did that. But I wish you weren't making a decision that looked so difficult. I think he has a lot of problems."

"If you'd been shot in the foot, you'd have problems, too."

"That's true," said Nancy Estritch, cautiously, "but let's discuss *why* he was shot in the foot."

"Oh, Mother," said Karen Estritch, "I knew you were going to bring that up."

CLAUDIA TOLD ALEX she didn't want to see him anymore.

She was upset about Lithuania. She imagined what it must have been like to have Soviet helicopters flying overhead, scattering leaflets inciting them to come back in the fold in what *Newsweek* called a "war of nerves" in what seemed to her an elaborate game of chicken played almost like a silent film, a game of chess, as down the street from the music conservatory an elaborate, almost baroque, piece of piano music played.

It seemed to her, it was all about who owned the nuclear power plant. Soviet troops had initially moved in to protect Soviet interest in the nuclear power plant.

She had read that morning in the *Wall Street Journal* that by the year 2000, the Soviet Union will have lost (conservative estimate) 283 billion dollars from the nuclear accident in Chernobyl and what Claudia didn't understand is, under the circumstances, why anyone would want to own a nuclear power plant at all. She knew it wasn't that simple, that it was one thing for Lithuania to declare independence but to annex all those Soviet businesses when they did was another issue, she just hoped it didn't all boil down to dollars and that the price of Lithuanian independence, if such a thing were possible, wasn't going to be Lithuanian national debt.

Claudia's lawyer had called that morning and told her she ought to think about filing for divorce. "At least file a legal separation," he said.

"Why?" said Claudia. "Is there a time limit on it?"

She didn't understand his answer. It had something to do with real estate prices dropping, the value of the house being less two years from now than it was now, the possibility that David's business was going down and the agency wouldn't be worth as much in two years as it would be in, say, a year. She had heard that David had lost a couple clients, but maybe he would gain a few. What the lawyer didn't understand was that it didn't matter to her.

"I try not to get involved," he said, "but it doesn't seem to me, Claudia, that you're having a *trial* separation, that either one of you is going to be smarter in a couple of months than you are now. I think, if I may say this, all it's doing is getting in the way of you getting on with your life." He sounded like Lucy. Was it that evident to everyone that she was stuck?

She felt like someone who was on a train that had been stopped in its tracks and, even though it wasn't a very liberated position, until someone came along and unstuck her (she hadn't thought that someone would be a divorce lawyer) she was just going to sit there on the tracks.

She thought about the people in Tiananmen Square.

She needed to file a legal separation. She was just putting off something that was inevitable like an operation that she knew she had to have. She called the lawyer back. "You're probably right," she said. "Go ahead."

The Lithuanian people had started to back down. They would not form their own border patrol. In an equal reconciliatory gesture, the Soviet Union offered amnesty from prosecution to Lithuanian deserters from the Soviet army but the Lithuanians still held to their right to self-determination.

She thought about the man in Tiananmen Square who stood before the tank.

The Soviets sent their own prosecutor to Vilnius, Lithuania. When the Lithuanians refused to work for him, the Soviets took over the prosecutor's office. A few hours later, the Soviets occupied the office of the central newspaper, as well. The Lithuanians requested recognition from the West.

If a tree falls in the forest and no one acknowledges it, does it make an official sound?

"ARE YOU SURE it isn't illegal?" said Lara Agnelli.

"Would we ask you to do something illegal?" said David Weiss looking at Mark Richards for back-up.

"Probably," said Lara Agnelli. She smiled at them.

∿∿

BILLY THOMAS realized it was the third time Lara Agnelli had called him. She was terribly sweet.

"Hi, Billy, are you better?"

He didn't know how to answer that. He had been told by his lawyer not to say that he was better but, of course, he was.

"Are you feeling stronger?"

"A little bit," said Billy Thomas.

"I'm so glad," said Lara Agnelli. "Eet really was terrible what happened to you."

Lara Agnelli understood him. She was an outsider, the same way he was.

"I want to ask you something, Billy. I have a film to start shooting in a month. A lot of it in a bathing suit . . ." she laughed.

"I can't, Lara," said Billy Thomas. "I know what you're going to ask me . . ."

"But I've gotten hooked," she said. "There's no one like you. I used to say this to David, the best thing he did was introduce me to you . . ."

"You and David are . . . ?"

"No more," said Lara Agnelli. "I cannot get between a man and his divorce." She laughed.

"I'm sorry," said Billy.

"I'm sorry for him," said Lara Agnelli.

Billy Thomas was sorry for him, too. Lara Agnelli was definitely worth holding on to.

"Billy, tell me what to do. I'm desperate. It's the first time I'll speak English. I have to look my best. Couldn't you just—supervise me? Sit down on the floor and tell me what to do. I have four weeks until we start. I'm so frightened of these other trainers," she said, "I will end up with muscles in my shoulders."

"Lara, I can't. I'm not supposed to. Would you promise that you never told anyone at all!"

⋙

"YOU CANNOT GET between a man and his divorce?" said David Weiss when she hung up the phone.

"I told you I was a very good actress," said Lara Agnelli. She smiled.

"FRANCIS HAS A FRIEND," said Lucy to Claudia. "Would you have dinner with us?"

It was only dinner. It wasn't a major commitment. And Lucy and Francis would be there, too.

"We thought we'd be grown-up and go out," said Lucy. "How's Tuesday?"

"All right," said Claudia. She had to meet David on Wednesday to discuss the details of their divorce and she didn't mind a night before that was grown-up and civilized.

The walls of the restaurant were gray. The tablecloths were charcoal colored with pale pink napkins folded into a fan. In the middle of the table was a basket of golden fries that looked like susie-q potatoes but was really a kind of whitefish supposedly the current rage in Japan.

Francis's friend whose name was Jacob was nice. He was a vet, not a G.I., an animal doctor, from New York who was checking out the possibility of moving to L.A. Claudia was his fifth blind date that week. She thought it was weird that he told her that.

Francis ordered the cheapest red wine on the menu and she and Lucy started laughing.

"It tastes all right. Doesn't it taste all right?" said Francis when it arrived at the table.

They had to admit it did.

Francis wanted to talk about Lithuania. "It's terrifying, don't you think?" he said to Claudia. He wanted to know if Claudia thought Gorbachev was going to invade. She didn't.

She ordered Pacific red snapper and tried not to think about the water quality of the Santa Monica Bay. It arrived with well-grilled radicchio. She hated grilled radicchio. She never could figure out how to say, "Hold the radicchio." David had always told her to think of it as garnish but it wasn't garnish, it was something on your plate you were supposed to eat.

"Do you think the French and Germans will persuade them to back down?" asked Francis. Claudia didn't. Although, she thought it was hard to say what the Lithuanians *were* going to do, as though they were their own version of an ecosphere, "If you cut us off," they seemed to say to the Soviets, "we will become a self-sustaining unit."

It was possible she had to move. David had mentioned something about selling the house and splitting the money which she hadn't wanted to think about at the time. And then move where? Probably to an apartment. There was something depressing about being a single mother with two children in an apartment.

She'd seen a report that afternoon on CNN of a demonstration in Vilnius, Lithuania, where thousands of people rode through the streets on bicycles—"If you won't give us gas," they seemed to say to the Soviets, "we don't care"—and where the bicycles stopped, thousands more stood in proud defiance in the Square as the Lithuanian National Orchestra conducted a perfect version of Beethoven's 9th, the Victory Symphony.

"The amazing thing about the Lithuanians," said Claudia, "is they don't seem frightened."

Jacob, the veterinarian, smiled and took another bite of his risotto.

CLAUDIA LOOKED at David's profile. He didn't look older than he had looked a year before. He looked less haggard, less rumpled. Successful. He didn't have that frantic edge he'd had, as though he'd barely had time to shave. They were sitting in her lawyer's office in a conference room with a wall of glass that looked onto another office building that was mostly glass in the middle of Century City. They were discussing how they were going to divide their things.

Claudia would get custody of Meggie and Rebecca. David would take them: every other week-end, for a month in the summer, and Thanksgiving or Christmas, her choice. That part was pretty civilized. The other stuff was a little sticky. The agency. David really felt the agency was his. And he had two partners. He was perfectly willing to give her half of his share but it was just that his share was so difficult to define. Her lawyer requested a copy of his client list but David didn't want to do that. He expected them to respect the privacy of his clients. Claudia understood that. Her lawyer didn't. As for the house, it was more difficult to divide. David's lawyer thought, basically, they should liquidate everything and divide the resulting cash in half but he understood if

Claudia didn't want to displace the children. "Divorces are unsettling enough." Her lawyer suggested that she could buy David out of his half. But his lawyer pointed out that then there would be capital gains for David. He wanted to amortize what the cost of the house would be if it were rented and charge her half of that for the months she had lived there without David. She decided to ignore them. There was a moment when the divorce and the disposition of the house were, basically, between her and David.

"Let me see if I've got this straight, David," said Claudia. "We can sell the house and each take half or I can buy you out of your half with the money I'm going to get from my half of your business. Is that right?"

"Sort of," said David.

"Think how complicated it would be if we had a summer house, too," said Claudia.

David smiled.

"I'll think about it," she said.

"Think about what?"

"Which one I want to do. If any," said Claudia.

The Lithuanians were still refusing to back down.

She had read that morning in the *New York Times* that a visitor had asked President Landsbergis if he recalled a Lithuanian folk tale that ends with an old man advising a youth, "Don't go through life asking for permission."

President Landsbergis smiled. "Oh, yes," he said. "I know it by heart."

Claudia didn't want to go home. She stood in the underground parking lot in Century City and wished she had somewhere else to go. She didn't want to go home. She didn't want to put Meggie and Rebecca to bed. Lourdes could do it alone tonight. Claudia had a ritual, each night after she read them a book, she would tell them a story about the day, what each of them had done that day.

Meggie went to school and played with her friend Katherine. Rebecca went to the park with Lourdes. Claudia went to her lawyer's office to discuss her divorce from their father.

She didn't want to tell them about her day.

She drove to the beach. There was a layer of smog out over the ocean. She'd never seen that before, almost like a line of brown above the sea. She stopped and had a drink at a place with sawdust on the floor and a view of the ocean. Everyone looked young at the bar. She drank a vodka tonic, which tasted to her like medicine. She walked to the parking lot and then realized there was nowhere that she had to be. The moon was almost full. There was a wind blowing offshore and the air was strangely clear and salty except for that thick layer of haze out at sea. She ignored the sign that said the beaches are closed from sundown and walked down the wooden steps to the sand. She took her shoes off and walked, she imagined it was a couple of miles, down the beach. The sun was setting and the sky was the color of pale pink roses. There was a milky pink and turquoise iridescence off the water, as though the ocean were made of mother of pearl. She could see the lights from the Santa Monica pier and something that she thought was Catalina in the distance. She imagined Meggie and Rebecca were asleep by now.

And then Mommy took a walk on the beach.

When she got home, she found, on her bedside table, a book Meggie had made in school.

A BOOK ABOUT ME

By Me Myself/Meggie Weiss

My name is Meggie___.

I am 4___ years old.

My hair is brown___.

My eyes are hazel___.

My favorite thing to do is Color___.

And then Claudia turned to the page where it said —

What do you want to be when you grow up? I don't know yet.

And Claudia knew she'd done everything wrong, not only was she subjecting her children to a divorce, they were also non-directional.

But then she turned the page and there was another page and, on it, was written —

Now, I know. I want to be a mother.

And all Claudia could think was, I hope you get the chance, Meggie.

She remembered a line from a speech she'd read that was given by an Indian named Chief Seattle 120 years ago. "We do not inherit this earth from our ancestors," he said, "we borrow it from our grandchildren."

D AVID CAME HOME to another message on his machine from the actress who owned the house he lived in, Sherry Edwards, who still wanted him to move. "Hi, David," that breathy voice like a cartoon character which made him almost insane, "it's Sherry Edwards. I hate to bother you. I just wondered if—you know how much I love the house." She didn't seem to care anymore if she actually spoke to David, she had entire conversations with his machine. "Kenny and I aren't going to get back together. We filed for divorce today, I guess you know that if you watched the news. And my series has been canceled." He was sorry about that. He liked her series. "Anyway, I know it's really awful of me to ask again . . ." she said. He turned the tape off before he heard the rest of her message.

He had had an awful day. He had left the lawyer's office where, finally, nothing had been settled with Claudia and gone back to his office to have a terrible fight with his partner.

His partner wanted him to sign Lara Agnelli as a client. Half the time he didn't know if he wanted to go out with Lara Agnelli and now his partner wanted him to sign her. It made sense, if Lara was going to start making 2 million dollars a picture, it was a lot of money even at 10%. 200 thousand dollars to be exact. But what if he wanted to stop seeing her? Or she stopped seeing him? On the other hand, Lara Agnelli *was* going to leave the agency she was with, IPA, and his agency *was* the logical place for her to go. But if he *was* going to sign her, shouldn't he wait until after the divorce? I mean, why should Claudia get half of the 10% he was going to make for representing Lara? Or maybe there was a kind of justice in that.

He had a headache that ran all the way down his shoulders. He turned on the jacuzzi and the bubbles started going. He loved the sound a jacuzzi made, there was something soothing about it, therapeutic. He waited 20 minutes for it to get hot. He took off his clothes, put on his bathing suit, and got into the jacuzzi. It was freezing. Was nothing in this house ever going to work? He was shivering. It was freezing cold outside, too, and for the first time, since he was about 4, he felt like crying.

"I DON'T KNOW WHY you're doing this," said Karen Estritch to Billy Thomas. "What has Lara Agnelli ever done for you?"

"You wouldn't understand," said Billy Thomas.

"I understand all right," said Karen. "It's this celebrity stuff. It's because she's a movie star."

"Don't you *ever* accuse me of that again!!" said Billy Thomas.

"I—I'm sorry," said Karen.

"You don't know who I am. You don't know *why* I do things. Celebrity stuff." He slammed his hand down on the glass coffee table and for a moment she thought it was going to shatter.

"I—I'm sorry," she said again. She shouldn't have said that to him. She knew it wasn't true. If it were true, how come he always talked about Seattle. They were going to move to Seattle when all this was through. "I'm sorry. I know you aren't like that," said Karen. "I guess I'm just"—she didn't know what to say to make it better—"jealous."

That stopped him. He smiled at her. "There's nothing to be jealous of, baby," he said. "Just don't say shit like that to me again."

LARA AGNELLI was wearing a white leotard, sleeveless, with thin straps that crossed in the back. She knew she looked fabulous with her dark hair pulled back and her neck arched like a thin Italian diva.

It was a hot day. Billy Thomas was wearing shorts. He walked with a cane and she could see that one leg was smaller than the other.

"Hi, Lara," he said, and smiled at her.

For a moment, she understood the attraction. There was something about his smile, those white teeth, broad shoulders, and he never did lose his tan. She suspected he went to one of those tanning windows, tanning booths, whatever they were, at the gym. She liked the idea of a drive-up tanning window except she knew David would think that was weird foreign humour. At least she could make fun of herself. She smiled back at Billy.

"You have to promise you won't tell anyone about this at all," he said.

"I promise," said Lara. "It's not my style to tell," she said.

"I guess I knew that," said Billy Thomas. He sat on the floor and she saw that he had trouble straightening his leg. "I'm not sure how this is going to work," he said.

"I exercise. You direct," said Lara. She smiled.

"I brought a tape," he said, and handed her a cassette.

"I'll put it on," said Lara. She felt as though she were involved in a seduction which in a way was true and she didn't know if it were going to take one session or more but she knew she was going to get him.

"I HAVE a very responsive body," Lara Agnelli said.

Billy Thomas could only imagine, although that wasn't what she'd meant. Lara Agnelli had said it in reply to his remark that her legs looked different in the three weeks that they had been working and she was able to do, with ease, an interesting version of the splits.

"I couldn't have done it without you," she said. She noticed that his leg was better. He'd managed to increase the size. He was sitting on the floor still but he was wearing shorts and she could see his legs were almost the same size again.

"Okay," said Billy as he snapped his fingers in time to the music, "keep pushing. I want you to really stretch. Over. And hands on the floor. Legs apart. I want this to *really* burn in the inner thigh. Two three four. Stretch. That's good now hands to one side. And over. Two three four. Stretch. Stretch. Good, Lara. On the floor, now. On your left side. Now right leg over your left leg and lift."

"I know I'm not doing this right, Billy," said Lara. "It's really easy."

"Keep your toe pointed down toward the floor." He illustrated. "Leg bent. And lift. Lift. Lift. Watch me."

She had him now. He was exercising.

"Oh," said Lara, "I can feel it now."

"Keep that toe pointed down," said Billy. "And all the way up. And all the way down. Five more," he said as he kept doing them himself in time to the music. "Three, two, one. How's that?" said Billy.

"I felt it," said Lara laughing.

"Now, on your feet," said Billy. And he got up, too. She had him.

BILLY THOMAS was alone in the conference room. The lights went down and he could hear the sound of rock music which he didn't realize at first was his exercise tape. The video screen started to flicker and a picture came on. *Lara Agnelli.* He had a terrible feeling he knew what was coming.

"I have a very responsive body," said Lara Agnelli.

"Okay," he heard himself say as he watched himself snap his fingers in time to the music. "Keep pushing. I want you to *really* stretch . . ."

He'd never noticed how artificial his voice sounded.

". . . Over. And hands on the floor. Legs apart. I want this to really burn in the inner thigh . . ."

How could he have been such a fool?

"I know I'm not doing this right, Billy," he heard Lara Agnelli say. "It's really easy."

He wanted to scream. *No! Stop!* He saw himself, from the floor, start to exercise with her.

"Three . . . two . . . one. How's that?" he said as he demonstrated.

"I felt it," said Lara laughing.

"Now, on your feet," said Billy. And he saw himself get up, too.

When the lights came on, Mark Richards and David Weiss were sitting across from him at the table. The video monitor was still on and there was that noise you get when the tape runs out.

"You should have accepted my offer," said Mark Richards, "when I offered you a hundred thousand dollars, you should have taken it."

Billy Thomas didn't answer.

"I don't think you want to go to court with me," said Mark Richards. "Do you, Billy?"

There was a really uncomfortable moment when Billy Thomas didn't answer and Mark Richards just kept staring at him, the white noise of the video monitor in the background.

"Sorry about your leg, old man," said Mark Richards. And he and David Weiss got up and left the room.

LUCY WAS REDECORATING. When Claudia walked into Lucy's living room, there were eight different patterns of chintz, excessive floral chintz, neatly pinned to the back of the love seat. There were eight different shades of green, polished cotton, linen, and sailcloth pinned to the back of the sofa. The back of the armchair was a mess, one floral chinoiserie, one deco chinoiserie, a multicolored striped design, three different darker shades of green, and a floral that was mostly white and beige.

"Maybe you should start with a new carpet," said Claudia.

"That's not funny," said Lucy. "Carpets are very hard to match. Do you think that the stripes look too masculine? Don't answer that," she said almost breathlessly. "Did you hear about Lara Agnelli and Billy Thomas?"

"*Not* really?!" said Claudia practically screaming the "not."

"No," said Lucy, "it's not what you're thinking. Apparently, David thought this up, your David. Lara Agnelli called Billy Thomas and told him there was no one like him and that she was starting a movie in a month — "

"Is that true?"

"What?" said Lucy.

"That she's starting a movie in a month?"

"Yeah," said Lucy, "that part's true. Anyway, she convinced him, it was her first English speaking part so, she had to look great. I guess, cause her English isn't that good. So, she convinced him to train her. Anyway, they taped him, they taped him training her, then, they showed him the tape . . . and, now he's had to drop his lawsuit."

"That's kind of amazing," said Claudia very quietly.

"It is amazing," said Lucy.

"I guess," said Claudia, "it also means that David's still seeing her."

"Lara Agnelli?"

"Yes," said Claudia, "Lara Agnelli."

"I thought you knew that," said Lucy.

"No," said Claudia. "I — I guess I should have known it." She laughed. "But I didn't."

"I'm sorry," said Lucy.

"Don't be," said Claudia. "It's sort of good I found this out. I think I like the white and beige floral one," she said without losing a beat.

"I don't know," said Lucy studying the fabric swatches she had carefully affixed to the back of the furniture. "I thought this would help me," she said, "but it's only made me more confused."

"I WOULD HAVE LIKED to have been there," said Jacqui Richards. She took another sip of white wine. It occurred to Claudia that she was slightly drunk. They were at an art opening in Santa Monica at a gallery with a large patio with no sculpture in it at all. "I would have liked to have seen his face when he saw that tape," said Jacqui.

"I can understand that," said Claudia. There were two men standing next to her speaking a language that she thought was Persian.

"You know, I *really* hate him!" said Jacqui.

What Claudia thought was interesting was that even when Jacqui was expressing an active, aggressive, intense dislike, her face retained a placid kewpie doll quality, as though she were just about to smile. "I can understand that, too," said Claudia.

"At first," said Jacqui, "I felt betrayed. And then, I was ashamed. And now, I just hate him. All in all," she said, "I think it's been a broadening experience." She smiled at the two Iranian gentlemen, who gave her a polite nod back, then she looked across the patio at Mark, before turning back to Claudia. "How's David?" she said.

"He's all right, I guess," said Claudia, who at this point wanted to go in and see the art even though it was terribly

minimalist, white paintings on white canvas, but someone told her if you stared at them long enough, you could
see every color in the rainbow.

"Don't you ever see him?" asked Jacqui.

"Sure, I see him, when he comes to get the kids," said
Claudia. "I was — I was thinking about going with him
to Meggie's school play this week."

That wasn't true. She hadn't been thinking about going
to Meggie's school play with David. But it had occurred
to her that it wasn't fair to Meggie that she always only
got one of them at a time.

D AVID PICKED CLAUDIA UP at home. He still hadn't had his car phone fixed and it rang once when he turned out of the driveway which made her smile. She asked him if he ever worried when he was stopped at an intersection that the person in the car next to him was going to pull a gun and he would be the victim of a driveby shooting? He said, "No, it never occurred to him," but that she had asked it made him smile. Meggie played a wood sprite and it was sort of in character that she kept on giggling.

Claudia had heard on the news that morning that they had discovered a mexfly (a mexfly is sort of like a medfly except from Mexico) in Los Angeles, actually, two mexflies, and it was announced that aerial spraying of the insecticide malathion would continue through the summer.

Mathew Horner's mother smiled at Claudia across the classroom. She couldn't tell if it was just a smile or one of those smiles like, "It's so great to see you back with your husband . . ." Mathew Horner played a tree that Meggie ran around. Claudia knew that Meggie sort of had a crush on him. Halfway through the performance, he fell down and someone in the audience, one of the parents, not Mathew Horner's parents or her or David, had the bad form to shout out, "Timber."

Someone had told her earlier that week that there was a medfly trap two blocks away in a tree at the top of a street called Lookout Mountain. She thought about taking it down but then it occurred to her they would probably just put it up somewhere else in a place that was harder to find. It would make more sense to empty it every week before they came to check if she could figure out a way to get up in the tree without getting caught. That would be embarrassing, to be caught in the top of a tree trying to empty a medfly trap. Or radical. But she couldn't find the trap and the person in the Laurel Canyon Neighborhood Association who'd told her about it to begin with couldn't remember which tree.

She didn't know how it had come to this, how anyone thought it was actually all right to fly over a city in a helicopter and drop malathion on everything that lay underneath. They actually said, "Cover your cars." Well, if it ruined the paint on the cars . . .

Meggie played a wood sprite and it was sort of in character that she kept on giggling.

∧∧

"DO YOU WANT to come in and help me put them to bed?" asked Claudia when David turned into the driveway and the car phone rang again.

David picked up the receiver and slammed it down. "I'd like that," he said.

LARA AGNELLI had been trying to reach David all day. She had called him in the morning in the office but his secretary said he was on the phone. When he didn't call back in two hours, she called again but the guy on the switchboard said David's secretary had gone to lunch and David had gone for the afternoon.

"I called earlier," said Lara Agnelli. "Do you think he got my message?"

"I'm sure he got your message, Miss Agnelli. Do you need one of the other partners?"

"No," said Lara. "Just leave word I called again."

She tried him in the car but she got that recording — "The mobile customer you are trying to reach is away from the car or out of our service area. Please try your call again later. Thank you."

She called him at home but David had canceled the answering service the week before because they never answered and the answering machine he'd installed didn't work — it answered and then there was a long space and then a series of little beeps which repeated about six times until it cut off and she got a dial tone. She tried it again and the same thing happened.

She thought about calling the office back, he'd probably check in, but she didn't want to appear hysterical. She was a little hysterical. She was leaving the next day for location and she was sort of wound-up. She had a wardrobe fitting in an hour. All this costume designer wanted to do was dress her in blacks and grays. She wanted color, something vibrant on the screen. She knew how she looked best. And they'd never changed that dialogue in the opening scene. And there was still a sex scene that was so graphic (and crude) that she would have to refuse to perform it, not that she wanted to appear difficult. She didn't think she should have to fight these battles herself. What did she pay him for? She didn't understand how David could disappear on her today. Maybe she *should* call one of the other partners. Or another agency. She tried him at home again and now the answering machine didn't answer at all.

She hung up the phone and it rang as soon as she set it down. It was Victor Sterrano, the director she'd worked for in Italy, the one who'd told her she could act to begin with.

"Oh, Victor," said Lara Agnelli, "you have incredibly good timing."

"Darling, I couldn't come without seeing you first thing. Can I take you for dinner tonight?"

"Oh, Victor," said Lara, "I'm so glad you're here. I'd love to have dinner with you tonight."

"I DON'T KNOW WHY you're so angry," said David to Lara Agnelli when he called her on the car phone from the curb outside of Claudia's.

"You didn't call me back," said Lara. "I left messages for you everywhere. I called you in the car. Somebody hung up on me."

He really needed to get his car phone fixed.

"We have a professional relationship, David."

"Professional" was one of those words that sounded very Italian when she said it. "I don't want to mix things," said David, "but I thought we had more than that."

"We have more than that, David. But I don't think it's wrong of me to want attention."

"I'm on my way —" said David.

"Here?" said Lara Agnelli.

"Do you want me to pick something up? Chinese food?"

"I'm on my way to dinner," said Lara Agnelli. "With Victor Sterrano."

There was a beat where David didn't say anything.

"It's only dinner, David. Don't you want to know why I was trying to reach you?"

"Shoot," said David.

"They never fixed that sex scene, David," said Lara Agnelli. "Will you call Brian [Brian was the director] and tell him I can't possibly show up on location unless you have his promise that it's going to be fixed. Will you call Jamison [Jamison was the studio executive] and tell him the same thing. I don't want to be difficult but — "

"Lara, don't worry. They promised to fix it, they'll fix it. Nobody's had time. When will you be home? I'll come by later."

"Oh, David," said Lara Agnelli, "I don't know if that's a good idea. My plane's at 8 in the morning."

"I see," said David.

"No, you don't see," said Lara, "I haven't finished packing. I want to study the script. Rehearsals start tomorrow night. I have to be in character. You're coming in 2 weeks, aren't you? I hear it's hot there. I hear there are a lot of bugs in Georgia," said Lara Agnelli.

"Only at night," said David. And he hung up the phone before she could say anything more.

David drove home and pressed the magic genie that opened the garage door but it didn't open. Actually, it opened, a little, about 4 inches, and just hung there making a terrible noise, like an electric crane that can't quite start itself, and wouldn't go up or down. He felt sort of stupid. He really hated this house.

"I'M NOT SURE you should give it up," said Kevin Baker, the real estate agent. "It's an 8 house."

"What's an *8* house?" said David Weiss.

"I never told you about this?" said Kevin Baker. "Every time I put a client in a house where the address adds up to 8, they get rich."

"What happens when they move?"

"It isn't pretty," said Kevin Baker. "One of them went broke, investment banker, real mess. One got *so* rich, she kept the house as an investment and moved to a bigger house so, that doesn't count. Another one got a terrible disease. You don't need more rooms. I wouldn't risk it."

"But nothing in the house works, Kevin."

"Things break," said Kevin Baker, "what can you do."

An oil tanker called the *Mega Borg* caught fire off the coast of Galveston and 89 million gallons of crude oil threatened to spill into the Gulf. In the three days before the fire was contained, the U.S. Coast Guard stood by and observed (a euphemism for watched). Claudia saw a Coast Guard spokesman on the news who said, "It is not our mandate to get involved in private disasters, the *Mega Borg* is privately owned." But, it seemed to Claudia, if 89 million gallons of crude (over 5 times the amount that spilled off the *Exxon Valdez*) were to spill into the Gulf of Mexico, it would be something *more* than a private disaster. It reminded her of her favorite thing about Ronald Reagan.

Her favorite thing about Ronald Reagan was: When Jimmy Carter was in the White House, he installed solar panels on the roof to heat the West Wing. When Ronald Reagan moved in, he equated solar energy with communism and took the solar panels down.

But the part that astonished her was, that it was 10 months after the *Exxon Valdez* ran aground in Alaska and the United States still had no formal plan, emergency response teams, or containment procedures in the event of a major oil spill.

JACQUI WANTED to know how they could tell if a medfly was sterile.

It was 8:30 in the morning and Claudia thought it was odd that *Jacqui* had called to talk about medflies. Or solicitous. But every time she thought she had Jacqui figured out, she turned out to be more complicated than she had thought. "They make them sterile," said Claudia. "They radiate them."

Meggie tapped her on the knee. "Just a second, Meggie," said Claudia. Meggie tapped her on the shoulder and held up a book. "I'll read to you in a second, honey," said Claudia, "as soon as I get off the phone."

"I thought it was bio-engineering or a birth defect," said Jacqui. "*How* do they do it?"

"With x-rays," said Claudia. "Poor things." She suddenly had an image of a hundred little medflies scrambling to put lead vests on.

"The male ones or the female ones?" said Jacqui.

"Males," said Claudia who actually knew about this because she'd read an article in the dentist's office. "Female medflies shut their reproductive systems down after mating once," she explained, "so, the thing is to get them to mate with sterile flies the one time they mate."

"Oh," said Jacqui. "I'm thinking about being tested."

Claudia didn't know what to say. Tested for what?

"Did you know Mark and I have been trying to have a baby?"

"I didn't know," said Claudia. "That's great. I guess that isn't great. I mean — "

"I know what you mean," said Jacqui. "You didn't know. We tried for almost a year before we split up. Now, we're trying again. Not that I mind. Who wants to get fat? And, we can always adopt. I'd feel good about that. We saw a lawyer yesterday who does those things. I'm just not sure I know what the rules of open adoption are."

Claudia laughed. "I saved some clothes," said Claudia, who didn't actually know if Jacqui would want her baby clothes.

"That's nice," said Jacqui. "Would you think it was odd if I was never tested? I mean, at least that way," said Jacqui, "if there *is* something wrong with me, I could keep the illusion that I'm perfect?"

Claudia didn't know if it was all right to laugh at that.

"Did you know," said Jacqui, "I read about it in the paper — that there's a shortage of sterile medflies in L.A.?"

"I read about that," said Claudia.

"What I don't understand," said Jacqui, sounding like herself again, "is why they don't just make more?"

"I'M GOING with him, Mom," said Karen Estritch. "And there's nothing you can say." She was loading up the red convertible mustang her father had given her for her birthday when her mother pulled into the driveway. The trunk was loaded with as many of her belongings as Karen could stuff in and some other items that didn't properly belong to her, cans of soup (at least Nancy didn't have to worry about her starving), the portable Sony CD player from the family room.

"Were you planning on saying goodbye?" She didn't sound angry when she said it, just hurt.

Karen looked embarrassed. "I — I was going to leave a note."

"Where? *Am* I allowed to ask where you're going?"

"Seattle," said Karen. "Billy has a job up there."

"Really?" said Nancy Estritch. "What about school?" She had an image of her daughter selling crystals in a New Age store, barefoot, with a piece of rawhide tied around one ankle, wearing something that looked like a caftan. This was hard. This was the hardest moment she'd ever had with her daughter. She couldn't imagine going up to visit her. She would have to buy a caftan, too, or at least a shawl and silver earrings made by an artisan.

Karen slammed the trunk of the red mustang and Nancy realized she was really going. "You can always come back, you know," she said. She thought about giving her daughter a hug but stopped short of that.

"WHERE HAVE YOU BEEN, David?!!" said Lara Agnelli. She had a kind of hysterical edge in her voice. "I left messages for you everywhere. I called you in the car. Somebody hung up on me."

He really needed a new car phone. "I was at Warner Brothers in a meeting."

"I can't do this, David. I really needed you today. I *need* somebody on the set. I *need* space. They want me to *share* a dressing room with Kathy Jamison. It's completely unacceptable. They told me I couldn't have my own make-up woman. I have to *share* her, too." When she said the word "share" she sounded very Italian and volatile. "It's too much for me, David. I don't feel taken care of — "

"It's okay, baby," said David, "I'll fly down tomorrow." It was 10:30 at night. He needed to send flowers, something exotic with lilies and orchids which would arrive in her room in the morning.

And then he wondered, If they were only friends would he send flowers or did it suddenly have more to do with their recently cemented agent/client relationship. He was actually working to calm her down.

"I hear you look beautiful in dailies," said David. There was a solicitous tone in his voice. It was sort of disgusting, and she was out of control. Lara liked to do that anyway. He remembered when she'd thrown her clothes all over the apartment and threatened to go back to Italy.

She had started to cry. Deep, racking, hysterical tears.

"Take a deep breath, sweetheart," said David. "It's okay."

She was sobbing now over the phone, uncontrollably, the way a small child would sob.

"Lara," said David, "it's going to be okay. You wanted this. Remember?"

IT WAS THE HOTTEST DAY that had ever been recorded in L.A. — 111 downtown. The temperature in
Phoenix, Arizona, reached 123.

Lucy called Claudia. "Do you think they miscalculated
global warming?"

"It's possible," said Claudia, who'd seen a piece in the
New York Times the day before that suggested that they
may have miscalculated ozone depletion, with a really
scary figure in it, like, 50% ozone depletion had been
recorded at one of the poles. They'd miscalculated the
Hubble telescope. She'd always thought they'd miscalculated over-population, the other way though, because
weren't we supposed to have run out of room already?
She *had* read somewhere that an effect of global warming
would be increased wind.

All night she'd heard the wind. Rebecca had crawled in
bed with her. "There's someone at my window, Mommy."

"It's all right, Rebecca, it's just the wind."

She and David were almost done. He was giving her the
house. The whole house. Clean. No buy out. And a third
of his share of the agency. He had offered her half but
Claudia hadn't felt that was fair. Her lawyer almost
popped a vein. "Why are you negotiating against your-
self?" he hissed.

"I don't think you want to have a political discussion with me," Claudia whispered back.

"Oh," said the lawyer, "I think I understand."

It was a lot of money as it turned out. Even by Jacqui Richards' standards — enough money to shop. The agency was doing well. Curious to think that, through this, she wouldn't have to struggle anymore. They'd always struggled.

It occurred to her that if they had stayed together, they would be rich, actually rich, and she wondered if that had occurred to David.

Probably he would be rich, anyway. After he married Lara Agnelli. She assumed he would. Marry her. And that it was something Meggie and Rebecca would get used to when they were sixteen or seventeen after they had given Lara Agnelli a really hard time for years. She wondered if she was going to learn to like to shop.

"S'hot, Mommy."

"I know it is, sweetheart. Just lie here under the sheet with me."

DavID THOUGHT it was sort of incredible that it was the hottest day of the year ("so far," Claudia would have said "it was the hottest day of the year . . . 'so far' ") and there had been a power failure in Laurel Canyon in the middle of the night. No lights. No air conditioning. No jacuzzi. For nine hours. And the stupidest part of all, he'd just bought these fancy new cordless phones which he'd been so pleased about, he could walk all over the house, but the damn things needed electricity to work, so, he couldn't even call anybody to complain. Not that there was anyone to call. God, it was hot. And there was that wind again. He wondered if it was just his hill that was windy.

KAREN ESTRITCH put her hand up to her eye. She could tell it was swollen. She shut her eyes but her head hurt just as much with her eyes shut as with them open. She felt sick from the pain and the heat. It was so hot her dad would say, "You could fry an egg on the sidewalk."

She looked around the apartment. Billy Thomas wasn't there. And then she realized, most of his things weren't there either. There were her suitcases on the floor, packed. Not his. The little desk was gone, the black butterfly chair in the living room. She didn't see her stereo. She figured out that he must have left for Seattle without her. She didn't know how she felt about that.

She remembered his blind rage before he hit her.

She felt like she had been drugged. She sort of remembered taking a pill after he hit her.

"Here," said Billy Thomas handing her a black pill and holding a glass of water up to her lips, "this'll make you feel better." And then he washed the cut around her eye with a cold wash cloth.

She put her hand up to her eye again. She didn't want to look in the mirror. She pulled her t-shirt over her head and stifled a small scream that came from her involuntarily. She felt like she might have cracked a rib. She struggled to put her jeans on. She put on her socks and her reeboks. She wanted to go home. She remembered what her mom had said. "You can always come back, you know."

GOD, IT WAS HOT. Jacqui Richards actually saw a bead of perspiration on her forehead. Mark was asleep. She didn't know how he could sleep in this heat. She probably should have gone to the doctor and had the test done in the office but she didn't think she could take the disappointment if they'd told her she wasn't pregnant. She felt like a specimen. She had peed into a little cup, poured the pee into a little glass tube which had something else in it, and now she was supposed to wait ten minutes. The bathroom felt like a sauna. It was so hot, the heat kind of seeped in the cracks of the windows and interfered with the air conditioning. This was taking too long. She made herself take deep breaths. It didn't work. There, that was long enough. There was this little strip of paper she was supposed to stick in, then wait some more. She started a bath and added some lavender bubble bath, bracing herself for disappointment.

She left the bathroom while the water ran. It was almost as hot in the bedroom even though the air conditioning was stronger in there. Mark was asleep on his side under the covers. He looked like a little boy. There was something so untroubled about the way he slept. She didn't know how he could sleep in this heat.

When she walked back in the bathroom, she took the little strip of paper out and ran it under cold water, like the instructions said, to see if it changed color. She was totally startled when it did.

She put her hand softly on her stomach. She turned to the side and looked at her profile in the mirror. That would be the end of her figure. She wondered if Mark was going to let her have a new trainer to help her get it back.

A SINGLE mated female medfly was trapped in a nectarine tree in Rosemead, just north of Interstate 10. California agriculture officials made plans to re-spray what had been one of the most heavily sprayed areas in the last year which would seem to indicate to Claudia and a few other isolated moms and environmentalists that there was some question as to whether aerial spraying of the insecticide, malathion, worked.

Her separation papers had arrived but she couldn't bring herself to sign them. She put them up on the bureau in her bedroom, high enough, she reasoned, so that Meggie and Rebecca couldn't find them (which made no sense since neither one of them could read).

Lucy would tell her she was having a hard time letting go. It wasn't that. It was that she had been taught not to sign anything unless she'd read it first and she couldn't bring herself to read these papers.

David had already signed. If she signed, it would be final. Claudia studied his signature to see if she could tell his mood when he signed.

The Lithuanians had declared a 100 day moratorium on their independence. In return, Gorbachev had lifted the oil embargo. She wondered what the mood was in Vilnius, Lithuania.

It WAS 7 in the morning. The house was quiet. David heard an owl outside his window.

The northern spotted owl was near extinction. He knew why — because it was in danger of losing its habitat.

He heard it again, that plaintive, low sound that wasn't like the sound of any other bird.

He looked around the house. It was terribly clean. Maria, the housekeeper had been there yesterday and the house was designed so that everything in the house had a place to be. There wasn't any clutter. Everything in the house worked now. The roof, the garage door. But the house was too quiet. It almost made him nervous.

He thought about his other house, if it still was his other house. Claudia had probably signed the papers by now. Meggie and Rebecca would be up. He imagined the sound of their feet padding down the hall. They were either giggling or screaming. They never just woke up. They either woke up and played or woke up and fought without too much in between until after they'd eaten breakfast. He never thought he would miss the noise.

Lara Agnelli was still away. They had discussed living together when she returned, in a bigger house with a pool, a house where the numbers also added up to 8 if

Kevin Baker could find it but David wasn't sure. There was something one-sided about their relationship, putting aside for a moment that he was her agent. There had always been rules. He remembered that night at the Swedish embassy when they'd run into Claudia and Lara had demanded that he take her home:

"I told you, David, I don't want to be part of this," she'd said.

"Part of what?"

"Part of your divorce," said Lara.

He couldn't remember if he had ever felt that she was there for him or, when she was actually there, how long she would stay. There was always the chance she would walk out, as she had that night, if Meggie didn't like her dinner.

God, the canyon was quiet in the morning. He didn't think any of his neighbors were up before noon. There was that owl again. He listened carefully. It was only one owl.

"IF YOU DON'T STOP bothering me, Rebecca," said Meggie, "I'm going to tell Mom." Meggie was sitting at the breakfast table trying to color a picture and Rebecca was poking her with Donatello, one of the plastic Teenage Mutant Ninja Turtle toys her father had given her last weekend.

"Cowabunga, dudes," said Rebecca, except it sounded more like "Calabung-a, doods" when she said it, which Claudia thought of as the California version.

"If you put your shoes on," said Claudia to both of them, "I'll take you to the park. Maybe we'll find some friends there."

"Okay," said Meggie, who ran upstairs to her bedroom with Rebecca right behind her.

Claudia called Lucy but no one was home. She thought she heard someone pull up. It was Saturday, Lourdes's day off and she hadn't made any plans. Maybe it was the gardener.

It was David.

"Were we expecting you?" said Claudia, who thought maybe she had her Saturdays confused.

"I don't know," said David, "were you?"

She didn't know how to answer that.

"Did you sign those papers?" said David.

"Oh," said Claudia, "you came for those papers."

"Not exactly," said David. "I came to ask you not to sign them."

Claudia didn't know what he meant by that.

"I called Sherry Edwards," said David, "and told her she could have her house back."

"Why did you do that?" said Claudia.

"I thought — I thought — maybe I could come home."

"That was a little presumptuous of you, David, wasn't it?" said Claudia.

"It was," said David. He couldn't help it that he smiled.

"Daddy!!" screamed Meggie, as she ran up and gave David a hug.

David and Claudia just kept looking at each other.

"Is Daddy coming to the park with us, Mommy?" said Meggie.

"I guess he is," said Claudia.

They all got into the jeep. David made a right turn out the driveway and the car phone rang once. He picked it up but nobody was there.

"You really should get that fixed," said Claudia.

January 1991

Soviet troops moved into Lithuania and Latvia.

In China, Wang Dan, the student leader of the 1989 uprising in Tiananmen Square, was tried in Beijing and sentenced to four years in prison.

But no one noticed because on January 16, at 4:58 Pacific Standard Time, the United States and its allies went to war against Iraq. An immediate side effect of the war was a catastrophic oil spill into the Persian Gulf. No sea life is expected to survive.